A Love Like This, Pt. 1

Also Available in this Series:

A Love Like This, Part 2
A Love of my Own
Audiogasmic: A Book of Love Poems

Chapter One

Serenity.

"Oh, my goodness! I'm so sorry!" I yelped, slamming the door shut and barreling down the hall, returning to the room where the charity event was being held. I nearly fell, as fast as I was trying to get away from what I just saw. Maya saw me rushing back, still carrying the two purses I was meant to lock up until the end of the night. I handed her the key, and she looked at me strangely. "The room was occupied. I'll just lock our purses in the trunk of my car."

"Renny! What happened? What did you see?" she asked, talking through her clenched teeth as she smiled. She wanted to know the tea but didn't want to appear too unprofessional.

"I'll tell you later," I said, exasperated. Maya gave me a look that said her curiosity wouldn't make it through the night. But for now, she had to wait. I exited the building to lock our purses in my trunk. Once I returned, a few minutes later, I was much more relaxed and ready to work.

"Thank you for helping me out again, girl. You wouldn't believe how hard it is to find people who actually want to work!" Maya said.

"You know I always got you. What do you need me to do first?" I asked

Amaya, or Maya for short, owned one of the best luxury catering companies in Charlotte, North Carolina, called *Le Fleur Catering & Events*. She started working in the industry when she and I were in college to make extra money, aside from doing hair in her dorm room. Soon, Maya realized she had a knack for the business and wanted to own her own catering company. During our sophomore year, she started working on her business plan and changed her major from mathematics education to become an elementary school teacher, to business management and entrepreneurship. By the time she graduated, she had earned enough seed money to get her business going. She started small, catering special events like baby showers and graduations. I helped her by working any event my schedule allowed. As her clientele grew, so did her business plan. Five years ago, her reputation and relentless work ethic got her the opportunity to cater one of the biggest weddings of the year between Mayor Sullivan and his second wife, Rebecca. The event went so well that she couldn't stop getting requests to cater major high-profile events throughout the city.

Tonight, was no exception. The annual *Keep Music in Public Schools* charity mixer was one of her biggest jobs to date. The event was sponsored by Infinity Records, who held the event every March. They are a well-known music label that produced many talented artists who had gone on to have successful careers. Honestly, even if she didn't need any extra help tonight, I was ready to volunteer! Who knew what celebrities would show up at these VIP events!

The large space for the event had undeniable vibes of luxury, elegance, and class. Majestic shades of purple and gold accents brightened the room; it looked regal. Maya had outdone herself this time. She made sure there were no details left untouched; from the custom printed gold silverware bands to the color coordinated water fountain with LED lights. The servers wore all black and were required to keep their hair pulled back off of their faces. Maya was particular about uniformity. Once the room filled to capacity, about 500 people, service was going smoothly. As Maya networked with people in the room, I served as her safety net, catching any issues the servers may have encountered.

Once we got over the hurdle of serving and clearing dinner, I relaxed and took in my surroundings. The room was full of musicians and entertainers I had been a fan of for years. I did my best not to be star-struck, but I had posters of some of these people on my walls when I was in high school! The night started to pick up when the musical performances began. By that time, Maya had relieved me of my duties. So, I could sit back and enjoy the show.

I was eating a piece of cake and swaying to the music when a gentleman sat next to me and said, "Hi."

I gave him a glance, a half-hearted smile, and replied, "Hello," still trying to enjoy the current performance.

"My name is Sean," he said over the music. "I think we met earlier." I frowned and turned to look him in the face. Suddenly, I realized he was one of the people I walked in on earlier when I went to lock up mine and Maya's purses.

My eyes stretched wide, and he had a silly-looking grin on his face. A handsome face, but silly, nonetheless. I looked him up and down. His navy-blue suit was perfectly tailored and looked like money on him. His cologne smelled marvelous. I'm sure his smile had gotten him through many doors that would have been closed to others. However, he did look a bit different without a woman in a sapphire blue dress glued between his hands, all but straddling him up against a wall. "Oh, um." I swallowed hard. "I didn't really see anything. I was just—"

"So, what's your name?" he interrupted. I didn't want to tell this man my name. If he got down like that in public places, I didn't even want to be seen next to him. I stood, "I'm Serenity James," I said, regretting giving him my full name out of sheer habit, due to my regular 9 to 5 occupation. "But I've got to go. It was nice to meet you, though, Sean." I scurried over to Maya, who thankfully was by herself.

"Girl, who was that fine man that you were just talking to?" she asked in a hushed tone.

I looked back over to Sean, whose eyes were still in my direction, "His name is Sean. I walked in on him and some woman earlier when I went to lock up our purses."

She raised her eyebrows. "They were in there …

you know—" I said, knowing she would get the hint.

"What?! With who? Where's the woman?" she asked, ready to gossip.

"I don't know; I haven't seen her. Thankfully, she didn't see me. Her back was to me. But if I do see her, I'll definitely be able to recognize that unmistakable sapphire blue dress she had on."

"So, what did he want?"

"I don't know. Probably to make sure I don't say anything about what I saw. But I don't have anything to say! It's not my business. As far as I'm concerned, I didn't see anything."

Maya went back to her business owner duties. I found myself a different spot to enjoy the rest of the performances. I was scrolling through my phone when I heard a familiar voice booming over the microphone. When I looked to the stage, I saw none other than Wesley Johnson, Jr., my favorite member of the male singing group called *Xtascy*. I hadn't seen him mingling with the other guests earlier. But I saw him now, and he looked just as good in person than he did on TV, if not better. He had to be in his mid-30s by now, and his group hadn't made any new music in a while.

Wesley greeted the crowd and thanked everyone for their donations. Before sitting down behind the piano, he gave a short speech about how important it was to keep the arts alive in public schools. I knew from the first note he played which song he was about to sing. It was one of Xtascy's love ballads called "Everything." I could still hear light chatter during his performance, but I was all in! My eyes were focused on him. I imagined he was singing it to me just as I did when he was my teenage crush. Maya rushed over to me. "Renny! I see you're watching your man sing to you!" she joked. We giggled like we were back to being those two teenage girls with nothing but boys and fashion on our minds. Once the song was over, everyone applauded, and he disappeared back into the crowd.

Maya's catering crew was loading up the equipment and finishing up for the night. There were five servers left to do the final clean-up. There was a local band on stage now to close out the remainder of the evening. "Are you going to try and get a picture with him?" Maya asked as she observed my eyes following him whenever he was in my view.

"You want to meet Wesley?" a man's voice asked from behind us. We both turned and looked to see it was Sean, the man I'd caught earlier in a compromising position. "I can introduce you," he offered.

Throughout the night, I had learned Sean was the VP of Marketing for Infinity Records. I began to say no, when Maya jumped in and said, "Yes! We would love to meet him!"

"Okay, I'll go get him. I'll be right back," he said, flashing a smile.

I turned to Maya and said, "I don't want that man doing us any favors!"

"Girl, please! What that man does behind closed doors is his business. Besides, this might be your only chance to meet him! He's right over there!" She was right. Sean's business was his business, and I at least wanted to get a picture.

I'm sure I looked a little rundown from working all night, but I didn't care. I got so nervous when I saw Sean walking back toward us with Wesley. *Damn, he's fine!*

Sean and Wesley came over to us. "Wesley, here's the two beautiful women I told you wanted to meet you. This is Serenity James, and this is …" realizing he hadn't gotten Maya's name, he paused.

Maya spoke up and said, "I'm Amaya Daniels, the owner of Le Fleur Catering & Events, and we are big fans of yours!"

Wesley's already present smile morphed into an even bigger one. Up close, he was a gorgeous man and was even taller than what I thought he was. He stood about six-three or four to my small five-three frame. He had rich chocolate skin, and a nice full beard that was neatly groomed. He was letting his hair grow out a little from his normal clean-cut image, and it was shaped into a tapered baby afro with soft curls. He wore a tailored all-black suit and a black silk shirt with the top two buttons undone. When I looked up at him, his trademark smokey gray-blue eyes almost demolished what little reserve I held onto.

"Amaya, it's nice to meet you. You've done an amazing job tonight! I'll definitely be giving you a call for my next event," he said, shaking her hand. He turned to shake my hand, "Serenity? That's a beautiful name."

I had to remember to breathe. "Thank you," I murmured, with a smile that could have been seen from here to Texas. "It's so nice to meet you, and you sounded incredible up there tonight!" I said, grabbing my confidence from thin air.

"I appreciate the love," he replied.

Just then, a gorgeous woman with long reddish-brown hair, light-golden skin, and an unmistakable sapphire blue dress came to Wesley's side. Intertwining her arm around his, seemingly marking her territory, she offered her lips to him for a kiss.

I looked at Sean. He stood there, appearing cooler and more confident than I expected. Seeing my eyes travel between the three, who were obviously in some type of secret love triangle only two of them knew about, Maya nudged me. "Wesley, would you mind taking a picture with us? Maya asked, interrupting the weird tension.

"Sure, no problem. Sean, do you mind?" he asked, motioning over to him to take the picture.

"Not at all."

I handed Sean my phone to take a picture of Maya and me with Wesley. Then Maya asked, "Can you take one more with just Serenity?"

He easily obliged. Candice Douglas, or the woman in the memorable blue dress, or the woman who was wrapped around Sean's waist just hours ago, watched us take our pictures with an arrogant smirk on her face. She was a former member of *Pretty Girl Gang's* singing group before venturing off to start her solo career. Candice told the media she wanted more creative freedom, however, her former group members said she was difficult to work with. I saw Maya look at me from the corner of my eye, seemingly wanting me to confirm what I'd told her earlier.

"Awe, babe, that's so nice of you to take pictures with the help," Candice remarked, placing her hand on Wesley's chest and fake smiling at Maya and me. Her comment wiped the smiles off of everyone's face, including Wesley's, who looked mortified. It was obvious that she was trying to be nasty. Why? I couldn't tell, especially since I now knew more about her than she realized. I guess she really hadn't seen my face when I walked in on her and Sean. Perhaps if she had, her attitude would have been a little bit nicer.

"I beg your pardon?" Maya spoke up, pushing her professionalism to the side. "The help?" she asked, ready to air the whole building out if need be.

"It's okay, Maya. Let's go. Wesley, it was nice meeting you, and thank you for the pictures," I said, getting us away from the whole messy situation.

Sean caught up with us and asked, "Serenity, can I talk to you for a minute?"

I knew he and I had nothing to talk about. I looked at Maya and said, "I'll meet you outside in a few minutes." I handed her my car keys.

"Okay, girl," was all she said before leaving.

"Listen, about what happened earlier, I would really appreciate it if you just kept that between us," Sean said.

"Us?" I countered. "Sean, I don't know you, and I don't know her." I nodded in Candice's direction. "I was just here to do a job, and now I'm leaving. I don't want any parts of whatever y'all have going on. So, there's no need for you to try to keep me quiet."

He looked relieved; like a relieved snake in the grass. "Okay, great." Sean pulled out a business card and offered it to me. "Call me sometime. You never know when you may need it."

This guy was a real piece of work. My eyes bounced from his face to the business card and back. I reluctantly took it, believing it would be the only way to end my conversation with him. "You have a good night, Sean," I said, not even attempting to act impressed.

Chapter Two

Wesley.
"Hey! Hey, excuse me! Miss Serenity!" I called out to her, trying to catch her before she made it to the lobby's front door. She turned around and looked stunned and almost scared that I was running up behind her. When I got over to her, she genuinely looked confused. "I'm sorry about what Candice said about you and Amaya. That wasn't okay, and her acting like that is not something I'm cool with."

She nodded and said, "Thank you for saying that, Wesley. I'm glad to see that you truly are a real gentleman. You're very kind. Hopefully, some of that will rub off on her," she continued in a low voice but loud enough for me to still hear. Now I was the one giving her a confused look. I had only known Serenity for five minutes, and that comment caught me off guard. I looked at her with furrowed eyebrows. "I'm sorry. I didn't mean to say that. It's

just—"

"Just what?" I pushed.

Serenity hesitated, then blurted, "She's not a good person. She doesn't deserve you. I think you can do much better." I raised my eyebrows at her boldness and candor, and before I could respond, she said, "Good night, Wesley," and left. *What did that mean?*

I returned to the main hall and found Candice. "Why would you be so rude to those women?" I asked, thoroughly irritated by her behavior. She sat there, looking in her compact mirror, touching up her makeup, basically ignoring my question. "Candice, you look fine," I said, closing her mirror. "Answer my question, please. Why did you say that?"

She huffed. "You take things too seriously. They were the help, and you're always too nice to everyone. It's okay to say no sometimes. You don't have to please everybody you meet," she answered, obnoxiously.

"Candice, I will never be rude to the people who supported my career. If you're going to be catty to every female fan I encounter, you can't come with me to events like this. You need to get your jealousy under control." I was visibly irritated, and she knew not to push me any further. Instead, she gave me the look she gives me when she wants me to forgive her. But it wasn't working tonight. It was time to go. "Candice, let me get you home," I said, ignoring her advances and finishing my club soda. "I'll pull the car around and meet you outside."

I got to the lobby of the building, and I realized Sean was supposed to be giving me a gift for my dad since he didn't make it out to the mixer this year. I was ready to leave, but I didn't want to make another trip back down here to get it, so I turned around to find him. He wasn't in the main hall, but I knew he couldn't be far. Instead of going on a manhunt, I saw the men's room and figured I'd stop in there real quick before I called him. I washed my hands and texted Candice that I'd meet her outside in a minute.

Before I could hit the button to call Sean, I saw shadows moving in my peripheral vision down the hall. I heard low giggling and voices coming from around the corner. Typically, I would just go about my business; but today, my gut told me to see who it was. I quietly walked down the short hallway as the whispers became louder. I stalled when I realized I knew who the voices belonged to. I gained my composure for a quick second before increasing my stride and laying my eyes on Sean and Candice. They were so wrapped up in one another that they hadn't even noticed my presence. His hands were palming her thighs under her dress, and her fingers gripped his neck while their tongues crashed together in an almost animalistic display of passion.

"So, this is how it is!" I yelled, scaring Sean and Candice from one another's embrace. They backed away from each other like they were strangers all of a sudden.

"Hey, man! It's not what it looks like!" That was Sean's weak attempt to explain the situation. Candice froze. If she could have disappeared into thin air, I'm sure she would have. I advanced toward Sean as he lifted his hands in surrender. Candice jumped in front of me, stopping me from reaching him. "Baby! Stop!" she yelled.

My eyes pierced down at her. "Baby?" I scoffed. "Candice, move!" I yelled, growing angrier by the second. I didn't want to put my hands on her, even to move her to the side because as angry as I was, I probably would have hurt her by accident. However, I would move her if she didn't get out of my way.

"He doesn't mean anything to me! I'm sorry! I love you! I love you, Wesley!" she cried.

"I'm sorry, man! Wesley, man, relax! Let's just talk about this!" Those were more of Sean's words that I didn't give a damn about right now.

"Talk? We don't have anything to talk about!" I looked down at Candice and said, "Candice, move out of my way!"

The commotion in the corner began to attract attention from the few people who were still in the building. Candice was still using her body to protect Sean from my reach, which pissed me off even more.

"Wes! What's going on, man?" A panicked voice behind me yelled. It was Darren, or D, as I've called him since we were kids. D's eyes quickly assessed the situation along with a few bystanders. He grabbed my shoulders and began to pull me in the opposite direction.

I snatched out of his grip, "Nah, man, I ain't going nowhere! Let me go!" Candice's perfectly applied makeup was now a smeared mess from her tears, and Sean's face still had a look of fear and caution.

"Come on, man, look at them! They aren't even worth your time!" D said, trying to be the voice of reason. "Come on," he said again.

I took a few deep breaths to help my rage subside as D's words resonated with me. I looked at a crying and nervous Candice. I had no sympathy for her, and I remained unmoved by her emotions. "We're done. Don't call me!"

She reached out to grab my arm, but I moved it before she made contact. "And don't put your hands on me!" I barked. I looked over at Sean, who was still pressed up against the wall so hard that I was sure his imprint would be left in it. I looked around to see there was a small crowd that had formed around the whole debacle. I pointed my index finger at Sean and thought better of saying anything else. I was sure the threats I had for him would have legal repercussions. D grabbed me and pulled me to leave again.

Sean looked over to an already humiliated Candice and said, "You ain't worth all of this," as he fixed his disheveled clothes.

D and I began walking away, "Wesley! Wait!" Candice called out toward my back. I stopped in my tracks, actually considering listening to her plea. I turned toward her, and she looked like a pretty mess. No attitude, no snarky remarks this time, nothing. She was completely at my mercy, and she knew it. "Candice, you got who you want," I said, motioning toward Sean.

For the night to have been going so well, it took only five seconds for everything to be turned upside down.

Chapter Three

Serenity. One Month Later.

I laid in my queen-sized bed while muted light from the sun began filtering through the blinds, slowly illuminating my bedroom. I deeply inhaled, holding my breath for just a second. Then I exhaled.

I turned to him, "Good morning," I said with a sweet smile, rubbing my eyes so I could get a better look at him.

"Good morning to you," he returned in a low groggy voice. He moved closer to me and I covered my mouth.

"I've got morning breath! And so do you! Move!" I laughed.

"You know I don't care about that," he said, pulling down his boxers and stimulating my center with his fingers. He lifted my shirt and his tongue found my nipples. I closed my eyes and enjoyed the pleasure he inflicted on me. Without another word, he laid on top of me and I wrapped my legs around his lean waist. He entered me with ease and held his eyes to mine as he stroked me. I loved mornings like this. I loved *him*.

"Tell me what I want to hear," he demanded as his pace quickened, and he pushed deeper. All I could do was moan, "You know what I want to hear. Say it, Serena!" he groaned in my ear.

"It belongs to you! It's yours!" I panted.

Beep! Beep! Beep! My alarm rudely woke me up. I grabbed my phone to stop the annoying sound of my morning wake-up call. The sun still filtered through my blinds, but the other side of my bed was empty and had been for the past year and a half. I didn't dream of my ex, Tony, often, but when I did my mind was sure to replay the times he brought me pleasure, not pain. I had tossed and turned all night, and I was tired, but I knew I had to start my day soon.

The time was now 7:00 a.m. Last night's racing thoughts about my last serious relationship and how far I've come had caught up to my early morning slumber. I shifted my focus to the text messages waiting for me. I unlocked my phone and yawned. The messages were from Maya.

Maya: *GM Renny! We get the final approval today! Are you ready?*
Me: *GM. Yes, I am if you are!*
Maya: *I'm ready to get this process over with!*
Me: *LOL! Yes! But I'm getting up now. I'll talk to you later.*
Maya: *Alright, girl. Later.*

Maya and I had been working for the last six months to secure the purchase of a commercial property downtown. We finally found a property that hadn't hit the market, courtesy of Maya's inside connections. It was a sweet deal and already had two paying tenants with one vacant space big enough for an office. The property housed a beauty salon and a luxury-style barbershop. Maya catered an event for a reputable bank and had become good friends with a commercial loan officer who helped us find the investment property.

At thirty-two years old, I worked as a full-time senior financial planner. Investing, taking calculated risks, and long-term financial planning was what I did daily. I not only gave excellent advice to my clients, but I also followed it. I graduated from college with close to no debt, thanks to scholarships, grants, and the foresight of my parents to have money set aside for my education. My investment portfolio already included two residential rental properties, both paid off and now served as straight monthly income. My own home was set to be paid off within the next year. I started saving and investing right out of college, and I was proud of the foundation I'd laid for myself.

Maya had always been an entrepreneur, so her income varied for several years. However, now that she was consistently making close to six figures annually from her catering company, she felt ready to start investing more. Of course, I had helped her set up a few accounts along the way, ensuring Maya at least had a retirement fund. But after seeing my success, she became interested in real estate. Commercial properties were a little bit different than what I was used to, though. This commercial property would add a $700,000 mortgage to our portfolios. We agreed to split the costs right down the middle and planned to pay it off in fifteen years or less.

As much as I wanted to lay around for a few extra minutes, I knew I had to get up. I sat on the edge of my bed, placing the palms of my hands at my side, on top of the mattress. Before standing, I opened my music app to start one of my many morning music playlists. After tidying up my bed sheets and comforter, I took a short walk to my ensuite bathroom and turned on my Bluetooth speaker. I got the first look of myself for the day in my large vanity-style mirror, then turned on the shower.

The sounds of smooth R&B voices crooned through my speaker, filling the spaces between my soft gray painted walls and white tiled floor. I'm a music junkie, but I remained loyal to classic R&B and soul music. I snapped my fingers and did a little two-step while walking back over to the mirror. I let out a note that was not so in tune with the song now playing, but it was my best attempt at pretending like I was a part of my own R&B singing group. I undressed, tossing my clothes in the nearby hamper while giving myself own little concert, complete with dance moves, high notes, and intense facial expressions to match the song.

I needed a morning shower to start my day. The hot water pelting against my body helped me relax, while the music helped to soothe my thoughts. The song playing now was called "All for You" by the group Xtascy, and the memory of meeting Wesley last month at the charity event entered my mind. The thought of that moment made me smile all over again. There were four members in their group: Johnny, Blue, Marcell, and Wesley. All of them could dance, sing, and were very easy on the eyes. Maya always teased me about my crush on Wesley. But that's all it was, a crush. All young girls had crushes on boys growing up, and Wesley was one of mine. Before I knew it, I found myself belting out the final chorus of the song, *"All I have is all for you. My heart and my soul are all for you. My love as a whole is all for you. A throne for my queen is all for you. Every part of me is all for you."*

After one more song played, I exited the shower, wrapping myself in an oversized white cotton towel. I finished up my morning hygiene routine by brushing my teeth, cleansing, and moisturizing my face before slathering a cocktail of lotion and coconut oil all over my body. I quickly dressed in a simple business casual look, applied a layer of mascara, eye shadow, and nude lip gloss to complete my simple beauty routine. My thick, long natural hair had been in four large twists pinned up underneath my silk hair bonnet overnight but hung past my shoulders when I took the pins down. After much trial and error, unraveling and fluffing out my hair to its desired shape and fullness had become an art I could now quickly master. I pulled my hair up into a nice, neat bun and let a couple of curly tendrils hang from the sides. To complete my look, I used a small soft bristle toothbrush to sculpt my natural baby hair with a dab of gel. Not too much, just a little to polish my look.

I gave my final look a nod of approval in the mirror before making my way to the kitchen for a light breakfast. By now, the time had reached 7:50 a.m., giving me just ten more minutes before it was time to walk out of the door. Music still played as I toasted a cinnamon raisin bagel and poured a fresh cup of coffee into a travel mug before heading toward the garage. I kept my purse and keys by the door to make mornings a bit easier. After arming my security alarm, I closed the door and got into my car. I transferred my morning playlist over to the modest speakers in my midnight blue Toyota Camry. It was not the newest car on the road. But it was reliable, and I outright owned it.

Fifteen minutes later, I parked in the middle of the lot like I normally did. Compared to my coworkers' cars, my Camry looked like it did not belong. There was a line of brand new, luxurious foreign cars that comprised the expensive landscape of the building. Their cars were nice. I just couldn't see myself paying $80,000 plus, for a vehicle that depreciated before I ever drove it off of the lot. Yeah, my little Cam-Cam would do me just fine, and with just over 100,000 miles, it ran like new.

I walked into the prestigious Truest Financial Firm building that had been my home since graduating from the University of North Carolina, Charlotte, almost ten years ago. I was fortunate enough to intern for them during my sophomore year, through earning my MBA. I was offered a job as an associate before graduating, and I was now a senior financial planner. I worked hard for my role, and it had paid off. Sharon Jacobs, one of the only African

American women at the firm, served as my mentor. Sharon's big, warm personality shined through the instant I met her. She always wore big, bold, bright prints on her small five-five frame. Her skin was the color of lightly toasted cashews, and she wore her hair in a jet black, short pixie cut. Her makeup was always flawless. Up to this day, I'd never seen her without a full set of perfectly manicured nails. Sharon taught me a lot about the job, but she taught me even more about holding my own in this male-dominated industry, which didn't consist of much cultural diversity. Over the years, she had become more like a second mom to me.

Upon walking into the building, I was acknowledged by Julian Brooks, one of our security guards on the main level. "Good morning, Ms. James," he greeted me with a confident and flirtatious smile.

"Good morning, Mr. Brooks," I returned with a nod and a smile of my own.

"Julian. You can call me Julian," he returned with a little chuckle. "We go through this at least three times a week, Ms. James," he said with a broad smile.

I paused in my tracks and returned his stare while he scanned my badge. "And just like I tell you every time, you can call me Serenity," I said, flirting back.

"Okay," he finally agreed. "Serenity, how are you on this beautiful Thursday morning?" he asked, never taking his gaze off of me.

"I'm good, Julian, and you?"

"I'm doing good." He paused and then added, "I'm doing great," eyeing me from head to toe with an even wider smile.

I blushed and looked down at my outfit: high-waisted, sage green palazzo pants, coupled with my tucked-in soft pink, short-sleeved cotton blouse, complimenting my golden-brown skin and navy heels. I began to walk down the hall, and while still in mid-stride, I turned back to him and replied, "That's good. I'll see you later."

"I hope you have a good day, Ms. Jay—Serenity," he corrected as his dark brown eyes pierced me.

"You, too, Julian," I said, taking another sip of my perfectly tempered coffee and pushing the up-arrow button for the elevator. After my interaction with Julian, I entered the elevator smiling, taking the time it took to get to the 4th floor to gush about him. *Today is going to be a good day*. I exited the elevator and headed to my office.

I had just finished a late lunch at my desk before having to meet with my three o'clock clients. They were a middle-aged couple who had inherited a small fortune from the estate of the wife's recently deceased mother. The money she inherited was a surprise. The couple had been a hard-working pair the majority of their lives while raising two children on modest salaries. This was their initial meeting, which was my favorite type of appointment. I got a chance to dig into the nuts and bolts of our firm's offerings and how we could partner with them to reach their financial goals. I also got a chance to determine if our firm and I were the right fit for them. I shined during these consultations, and it wasn't too often I didn't gain a loyal client proceeding my presentation.

After about an hour-and-a-half, the couple left my office with lots of information and a retirement plan I had laid out for them. I had more satisfied clients. *I love my job*.

While finishing up some final paperwork, the end of the workday was sneaking up on me. It was a quarter to five o'clock. I had established a habit of leaving work on time to enjoy "me" time and get some proper rest. I looked down at my phone for the hundredth time today and realized I hadn't gotten the call I'd been waiting for since this morning. I hadn't heard anything from Maya, either. I was locking up my desk when I heard a light knock on my open door. I looked up to see a smiling Julian, which instantly made me smile.

"Serenity," he said.

"Hi, Julian." Then silence. Radio silence. I swear I could have heard a pin drop as quiet as the room got. I stared at him with half of a smile and asked, "Are you alright?"

"Yeah, yeah," he said, stumbling while clearing his throat.

I continued locking up documents, slipped on my shoes that I often kicked off under my desk, and grabbed my purse. Once I was standing to leave, Julian still hadn't uttered another word. He just looked at me. "Is there something you needed, Julian?" I asked with a warm smile, trying to calm his shaken nerves.

"No. I mean, yes. I mean — Uh, can I walk you to your car?" he settled on asking.

"Sure," I answered, looking at my watch. "You've got perfect timing."

Our short walk to the elevator was silent. Once the doors opened, he politely said, "After you," and stepped in behind me.

As we descended to the lobby, I asked, "Did you have a good day?"

Letting out a breath, it seemed like he was holding in, he answered, "Yeah, yeah. It was good."

It was clear that Julian had something on his mind he wanted to say, but he was too nervous to say it. I was a little taken aback by his behavior. He usually greeted me every morning with confidence, a smile, and a little flirtation for the past few months he had been with the company. I kind of thought he liked me, but I had witnessed him putting on the same charm for other women at the firm. So, I just thought he was a big flirt. Still, this man I saw now was unrecognizable compared to who I thought he was.

Once we got to my car, I said, "Thank you for walking me. It was very sweet."

"It's no problem," he said. Then he became quiet again. I questionably looked at him, and then I abruptly said, "Okay, then, well, you have a good night. I'll see you in the morning."

I pressed my remote to unlock my door. Just as I was reaching to open it, Julian blurted out, "Can I call you sometime?"

My eyes met his as he anticipated my answer. "Sure," I said, showing a glowing smile.

"Okay, cool," he said, sounding more like his normal self.

"What's your number?" I asked. "I'll call you right now so you can have mine," I said, holding up my phone. After giving me his number, I called him. He then opened my car door for me and asked me to text him when I got home safely. I thought that was very…thoughtful.
He closed the door once I was tucked inside, and we parted ways.

He asked me to text him to let him know when I got home safely, and I thought that was thoughtful.

Once I got home, I plopped down on the couch and kicked off my shoes. I picked up my phone to text Julian that I'd made it home. He quickly responded with, "Okay, have a good night. See you tomorrow."

"You, too," I typed. I put my phone down to go and change my clothes into some comfortable sweats and fluffy slippers. I also washed my face and twisted my hair into four large sections before putting on my multicolored silk scarf. I had some leftover chicken and broccoli pasta alfredo from the previous night that I heated before returning to the couch with a glass of water with lemon. I turned on the TV to catch up on some trashy reality shows I loved to watch. I didn't know why I liked them, but they were my guilty pleasure. Right before I began to let my thoughts drift into the unknown, my phone started ringing. Foolishly, I thought it was Julian, but it was Maya. I swiped right and said, "Hello?"

We talked about our day for a few minutes before discussing business. Maya said she had to submit more paperwork today for our loan application to get it approved. She assured me everything would be finalized tomorrow. Maya took charge of this process because she typically had more free time during the day and communicated more freely. I told her about Julian asking for my number. She seemed excited that I interacted with someone of the opposite sex. She was single, too, but she was actively dating. As for myself, I hadn't been interested in getting to know someone new for a while. Maybe it was time to change that. Maybe Julian would be worth the change.

Chapter Four

Wesley.

The morning always came too quickly for me. I was a night owl, suffering from a severe case of insomnia. When my alarm sounded at seven o'clock, I had been asleep for maybe two full hours. Knowing I had to meet with my dad at nine for breakfast was the only thing motivating me to get moving. Unfortunately, when I closed my eyes for what I thought would be another five minutes, I ended up being asleep for another hour and ten minutes.

Damn! I jolted out of bed, running to the bathroom to start getting ready. After draining my bladder, I discarded my boxers in a corner on the floor of my massive space, where other dirty laundry started to form a large pile. I jumped in the shower before turning the water on, only to be doused with a stream of cold water when I turned the knob. I sighed as I shivered under the cold stream for about ten seconds as it began to heat up. I did quick work of washing up and finishing my hygiene routine.

My dry cleaning had come in on Tuesday. It was no problem to pull a simple, all-black outfit together. I didn't waste any time with jewelry or cologne; I just needed to get out of the door. I grabbed a pair of aviator-style Ray-Ban's, my wallet, and keys and headed out the door. As soon as I got to my car, I realized I had left my phone upstairs on my nightstand. I blew out a heavy breath before marching back into the house, up the stairs, and snatching my phone from where I had left it. I saw that my dad had sent me a text five minutes ago at 8:43 :

Pop: *Son, are you on your way?*
Me: *Yeah, I woke up late. On my way now.*

Pop: *Ok, I got us our regular booth. See you when you get here.*
I guess it was a good thing I had to go back into the house because I realized I hadn't set my security alarm.

Thankfully, the little breakfast spot my dad and I frequented for the past few years, Sasha's, was only a ten-minute drive from my house, fifteen minutes with traffic. And, of course, there was traffic. That's just the type of morning I was having. I spotted my dad upon walking into the restaurant. He was seated with a cup of coffee and a newspaper. Yes, a newspaper. I could never figure out where he even found newspapers these days, but there he was just reading away like it was a feed on Instagram.

I sat down with a heavy sigh and said, "Hey, Pop, sorry for being late." I situated myself on the opposite side of the booth.

"Hey, Son. Late night?" he asked, still eyeing his daily read.

"Yeah, something like that," I mumbled as I looked over the menu I now knew like the back of my hand.

"Oh, really?" he returned with a look of interest while folding the newspaper in half and placing it on the table. "What's her name?"

"Man, Pop, it ain't even like that," I said, without really wanting to engage further in that line of questioning.

"Okay, Son," he said, backing off. "How have you been?"

"Good," I replied, still searching the menu.

Just then, our waitress arrived at our booth, placed a fresh cup of coffee in front of me, and offered Dad a refill. "Are you gentlemen going to have the usual today?" she asked.

"I will, thank you," Dad piped up.

"Uh. Hmm. I want to try something different this time," I said, still studying my options. Dad and the waitress looked at each other as if on cue and shared a small laugh.

"What's funny?" I asked, trying to find the amusement.

"You do the same thing every time we're here and end up getting the same thing, Son," he answered. After a moment of hesitation, I put the menu down and said with embarrassment, "I'll have the usual."

While sipping my coffee, Dad and I engaged in small conversations before discussing what we met once a month to discuss: business. Our food quickly came, and it was just as delicious as always. I always ordered the southwest omelet with sliced avocado and tomatoes on the side. Dad was a steak and eggs type of dude, so that's what he had. "I was talking to Trevor, and he said he's getting ready to leave his firm. He says he's been getting offers from other places around the city. Apparently, he's not happy with the way the executive team has been handling a few internal issues," Dad explained.

Trevor was Dad's and my financial planner. He had been a part of our lives for so long that he was more like a family member. "Like what?" I asked.

"Well, you know he's been with his firm for the past twenty-plus years. He says they've hired many new associates, who have made no secret of trying to poach his longtime loyal clients behind his back. Even at his level, and with all of the millions of dollars he's brought into the company, the VP's have done little to nothing to handle his complaints. I knew something was wrong when someone I didn't know called me just to "check-in," he said, using his fingers as quotation marks.

"Really?" I said in surprise.

"We're meeting with him in the next week or so. I will send you the details when I get them," Dad said, taking another sip of his coffee.

"Oh, my goodness!" Dad and I heard a woman's voice exclaim from across the restaurant. "Are you? Is that Wesley Johnson Sr. from the Midnight Stars?" Dad and I met eyes and then looked back over to the woman, who was obviously in shock.

"Yes, it's me," Dad smoothly said. I rolled my eyes and chuckled because I already knew what was coming next. The woman got up from her table and began walking over to our booth, phone in hand, before the owner of the establishment, Sasha, nicely stopped her and asked her to let us have our privacy. Dad, however, got up and walked over to Sasha and the woman and began saying something I couldn't quite make out. Soon after, Sasha returned to the kitchen as the excited fan melted over Pops while he engaged her in a friendly conversation.

I swear I heard him singing a few lines of one of his group's biggest hits, "Black Dress," to his excited fan. After giving her a friendly hug and taking a couple of selfies, he came back to our table while the woman looked as if she had just experienced her own little slice of heaven. When Dad sat back down, I just looked at him and shook my head.

"What?" he asked, with the biggest smile I'd ever seen him wear.

"Nothing, Pop. You good," I said, laughing.

"See, Son, that's what good music does. Even thirty some odd years later, people still feel good about the music we made even before you were born."

I shook my head, agreeing with him as he continued, "You and those boys have a legacy, too …"

I quickly cut him off. "Naw, Pop, we ain't talking about that again. The group was cool, but we had too many issues. I don't even talk to the fellas much anymore."

We picked back up on our conversation about Trevor. I didn't have any objections to following Trevor wherever he went. After all, he had taken good care of my family and me over the years. When I was making money from my singing group back in the day, the investments he made for me had done me well. While the guys in my group were buying diamonds, cars, and taking exotic trips, I invested almost 90 percent of my income to set me up for the long run. I did buy a few big-ticket, unnecessary items when I got my first $100,000 advance like any seventeen-year-old young man would with that much of his own money. Dad let me have my fun, for like the first year, then he had me meet with Trevor shortly after I turned eighteen.

Trevor taught me about investing and planning for my future. Dad instilled in me how fickle the music industry is and that, one day, the money I made had to last me for years to come. Growing up, I didn't want for much since Dad had been well into making money from his successful singing career. Once I started making my own money, I no longer let Dad support me financially, though he did give me a big lump sum of money when I turned twenty-five. He said he had been saving it for me since the day I was born and wanted me to have it. I took the money and, eventually, built myself the house of my dreams a few years ago and invested the rest. With Trevor's guidance, investments, and planning, I'm pretty much financially set for life. Even though I didn't perform anymore, I still wrote songs and produced other artists in the industry. The power and longevity in the music business were in the pen.

After I stopped making music with my group, writing had become my largest source of income. My dad taught me a lot about the industry before I even considered music as a career. He taught me the importance of writing and owning my own music, and his advice paid off.

*** * * * ***

After breakfast with Pops, I ran a few errands and made my way back home. I ended up taking a much-needed nap that lasted a little longer than I meant for it to. It was almost seven o'clock by the time I woke up. I was so tired that I fell asleep on the couch, fully clothed. I opened my phone and ordered some Chinese food to be delivered. Not only was I still tired, but I was also starving. While I waited for my food to arrive, I noticed I had five unread text messages. I opened the messages to see they were all from Candice. I hadn't talked to her since the charity event, but she did text me from time to time. I never responded, though.

Candy: *Hey. I need to talk to you. Call me when you get this (2:33 pm).*

Candy: *Hello?????? (2:50 pm).*

Candy: *I really need to talk to you. It's important, call me (3:18 pm).*

Candy: *How long are you going to ignore me? I said I was sorry! We've been through too much for it to end the way it did. (4:48 pm).*

Candy: *Look, I'm sorry about what happened. I love you. I miss you. Please, don't leave me out here like this. I need you. Please call me. I just want to talk (6:36 pm).*

Candice and I had been together for almost a year before I got a chance to see who she really was. I met her at last year's charity event. She was a part of a girl group whose first single landed them in the top ten on the Billboard charts. They had a few songs that charted afterward and became a recognizable name. After they finished touring for their second album, the group broke up. There were many rumors about why they split, but that was between Candice and her group members. The music industry is cutthroat; I should know. I kind of kept my eye on her during her career and had seen her doing interviews and performances online. But when I saw her in person, she checked all the boxes of everything I liked to see on a woman.

She was so damn beautiful. She had smooth light-brown skin; like when you spill a little too much creamer in your coffee. Her hair was reddish-brown and cut into a shoulder-length bob. She stood about five-five to my six-four and was thick and curvy in all the right places. But what really did it for me was the skin-tight black dress she wore and those thigh-high, snake-skinned boots she wore when we met. Candice's boots looked like they were painted on those luscious legs of hers. She was a stunner, a vision. Every man at the mixer that night, single and otherwise taken, swarmed around her the whole evening. I mingled with old friends, but my eyes found her wherever she went. It wasn't until I caught Candice in a rare moment by herself that I was able to approach her. When I went to introduce myself, she politely stopped me and said, "I know who you are. You're Wesley Johnson. I'm Candice." Our eyes locked, and she had me from that moment.

Things between Candice and I weren't always perfect, but I felt like it was always real. My shine from being in the spotlight had dimmed quite a bit by the time I met her, and I was okay with that. I enjoyed living a low-key life outside of the industry. Her popularity was still fresh, though. She still wanted to be seen, and that didn't really bother me. I understood. She had to play the game and build her brand; I got it. I wasn't opposed to her posting pics of her and me on Instagram, Twitter, and wherever else she had a following. She was working on her solo career, and from what she had let me listen to, she was putting together a solid project, so she needed to stay engaged with her fans. I gave her feedback and advice whenever she asked. But for the most part, she did her own thing.

Candice did have a bit of a jealousy issue within our relationship. At first, I thought it was because she was a little younger than me and still needed a bit more maturing. Over time, I noticed her interactions with women who approached me became more and more of a problem for her. It was a part of her personality I didn't like but dealt with because I deeply cared about her. I made it my mission to let her know she was the only woman I had eyes for; only her insecurities would not let her believe that. Our relationship had gotten to the point of just being a routine. I wasn't truly happy anymore, and I believed we were just on autopilot. However, I never thought about stepping out on her. I wasn't a cheater; that was something I would never do.

The day of the charity event last month, or the day I caught her pressed up in the corner with Sean, we had a big argument in the car on the way to the venue. She was upset because I wouldn't buy her some ridiculously priced designer handbag that had been trending online. I wasn't cheap. I often bought her expensive gifts, but she was almost throwing a tantrum over me telling her no. I knew our relationship was beyond repair. We had different ideas of showing love and affection, and I really saw just how selfish she was. I intended to end things with her that night, but she beat me to it. After the breakup, social media mentioned it a few times, along with speculations about what happened, but I ignored it. I learned from Dad a long time ago which battles to fight and which ones to let ride out. This one was going to have to ride out.

One thing that continued to stand out from that night was the woman, Serenity James, I had met. She said Candice wasn't a good person and didn't deserve me. Her words had echoed in my mind through many nights, and I found myself restless. The look in her eyes was so sincere that it silenced me. I know Candice was rude to her and her friend by making that comment, but that wasn't a statement someone who you'd just met made to you without a good reason, right?

Now, Candice was on my phone again, probably thinking I just needed some time to cool off. She was wrong. I should have blocked her when everything happened, yet a part of me wanted to see how she would answer for her scandalous actions. My fingers danced over the phone while I tried to decide what to respond or if I should respond at all. Back in the day, my group members and I had our pick of the pack when it came to women, and we picked often. Being young, black, attractive, and paid was the perfect combination to keep my bed occupied with the most beautiful women I had ever seen. I'll admit that I was a bit of a playboy back then. Even now, I didn't have any problems finding a woman to come through to keep me company.

However, at thirty-five years old, I was not interested in playing young man games anymore. Those days were over. Before I met Candice, I had been happily single for six months. Yes, I had called on a few after midnight acquaintances along the way to come through, but Candice made me feel like I could really do this love thing. I loved her, or at least I wanted to love her, and she made me believe she really loved me. I felt stupid for how things ended. I was mad as hell, but I knew I had to let it go. I deleted her texts and the last few pictures of her that remained on my phone and blocked her number.

The doorbell rang. I opened the security app on my phone to see it was my food delivery guy waiting outside. I grabbed my food, set myself up on the couch, turned on Netflix, and attempted to empty my mind from the thoughts of Candice. I saw my boy D had hit me up, but I didn't feel like talking. It was almost 9:00 p.m. when I found myself heading to my music room. The space was filled with plaques, awards, and pictures from the days the fellas and I were in our prime. I also had a keyboard, a couple of guitars, and some recording equipment in there. I needed to get my thoughts out. I needed to dull this ache I didn't want to admit I'd been feeling for the past month. I needed to filter the last thoughts of Candice out of my mind. After tonight, I decided she would be a distant memory.

After warming up my keyboard with a few chords, I began singing and freestyling a song. By the end of the night, I ended up playing and singing many songs. Somewhere in the mix, I pressed record before belting out one of my all-time favorite songs by my absolute favorite artist still living, titled "Lately" by Stevie Wonder. That was the song I sang for Dad as a kid that made him realize I actually had some vocal talent. Singing this song now held such a different meaning, though. I felt it. Maybe a little too much when I sang the lines about saying goodbye at the end of the song. By the time I was done in my music room, I looked at the clock, and it read 1:13 a.m. Once I made it to my bedroom and laid down, sleep found me almost instantly.

Chapter Five

Serenity.

It had been three weeks since Maya and I closed on the commercial property downtown. Today was the first time we were going to meet our tenants in person. Up until this point, all of our correspondence had been through email. It was a warm and sunny Saturday afternoon in the city; toes out weather, as I called it. Because I knew our visit would be more casual than business, I decided to wear a nice coral maxi sundress and sandals coupled with a light fabric cardigan that I rolled up to my elbows. I didn't often let my hair flow wild, but today, I was feelin' myself, and my twistout was everything when I took it down this morning. I made a side part and slicked back my edges a little bit, and my hair flowed midway down my back. I wore dark Tori Burch shades and diamond stud earrings, a gift from my father, and an off-brand purse that looked designer, but I picked it up at Target. Maya arrived a few minutes after me in her money-green baby BMW.

Unlike me, Maya spent her money on all the luxuries she could afford. She was a natural-born hustler and picked up side gigs whenever she could to make additional money. I could hear her now, "It's not like you can take your money with you, so you better spend it while you can!" She didn't live above her means; Maya just worked hard to get the things she really wanted.

"Okay, Renny!" Maya greeted me. "Hair out, legs out, skin poppin'! I see you, girl!"

I laughed. Maya stayed hyping me up on my looks, but she was a completely natural beauty. She made looking good effortless. If I woke up like this were a person, that would be Maya. Her outfit matched my casual energy as if we had planned it.

Maya stood about five-five with a peanut butter brown complexion, hazel eyes, and bone straight jet-black hair that laid just past her shoulders. She would be best described as slim-thick. She wore dark blue skinny jeans, a navy short-sleeved top with beading around the neckline, and a modest pair of heels that wouldn't hurt her feet. She had on a pair of oversized sunglasses, some brand-name purse, and her signature mid-length, red coffin-style nails. I looked her up and down and said, "Girl, I'm just tryna keep up with you! Go ahead and walk for me!" Turning it into a little impromptu song, I sang, "Go ahead and walk for me! Now turn it around, walk back to me! Put your hands to the ground! Make that booty talk to me!"

Maya almost complied with the song; except she didn't put her hands to the ground. That didn't stop me from serving as her hype-woman, though. That was okay. I mean, we were in front of our new tenants' storefronts.

Our first visit was to the hair salon, *A Cut Above*, to meet Jasmine, the owner. The reception desk was sleek and modern, and the space was bright and open. They offered courtesy bottles of water and beauty magazines to waiting clients. In addition to hair, their services included eyebrow tinting, lash extensions, and mini facials. Eight stations had privacy walls between the stylists. Jasmine and all stylists had clients in their chairs, but everyone still took a moment to meet us. "You have a beautiful head of hair!" One of the stylists complimented me. "Whatever your regimen is, keep doing it, honey, because it's working for you!"

"Thank you," I said, feeling a little shy. After doing a self-tour of the salon and leaving Jasmine our contact info, Maya and I decided to meet our other tenant next door.

Darren Wilkes, the owner of *The Gentleman's Luxury Barbershop*, was who we were meeting next. As we approached the entrance, I soon began to think two women going into a barbershop on a Saturday morning might be a little uncomfortable. Barbershops were painted with the stereotype of men not controlling their testosterone from boiling over when pretty women came in. However, when we entered, it was calm and unexpectedly quiet. There was a nice vibe going, and the energy felt serene. The space had mahogany hardwood floors and three stations on each side of the room. There was a small waiting area at the front of the shop full of patrons waiting their turn. The space was wide open, with large African artwork adorning the walls.

A tall, attractive, dark chocolate-skinned man with dark auburn eyes emerged from the back of the shop, smiling as he approached us. He had on a tight black t-shirt that had the name of the shop written across the chest. Speaking of that shirt, it left little to the imagination about how defined his muscles were underneath. His hair was styled in neatly groomed locs pulled away from his handsome face into a ponytail that reached a little past his midback. I couldn't forget to mention the tattoos on his neck and hands and his perfectly groomed goatee he stroked as he stood in front of us. Maya and I went silent. I know what I was thinking, so I knew what she was thinking, too. *Daaammmnnnn!* Men as fine as this didn't just work in barbershops; they graced the covers of magazines!

"So, you two must be my dancers?" The man asked with a wide smile. *Lord, and his teeth are pretty and white, too?*

"Excuse me?" Maya asked, trying to play it cool. I could hear chuckles from the customers waiting to the right of us. "Dancers?" Maya continued, confused.

"Didn't I see you two out there about twenty-five minutes ago dancing in front of the shop?" he asked with a chuckle.

"Oh. Well, yeah, I mean," Maya mumbled.

"We were just having a little fun," I said, jumping in to save my friend, who was drawn in by the charm of this man.

"No worries, we enjoyed the show," he said, still amused. His laughter was accompanied by several people in the shop, including two female barbers I was glad to see. *Is Maya blushing? I have never seen her blush or at a loss for words, for that matter, though I 110% understand it at this moment.*

"We're here to meet with Darren Wilkes," I said to get us back on track.

"That's me; I'm Darren," he replied, glancing at me but returning his eyes to Maya even quicker. Obviously, she was smitten by the attractive stranger.

"I'm Serenity James, and this is Amaya Daniels. We're the new landlords. We've emailed you a few times to let you know we were coming today. I'm not sure if you got them," I said, attempting to give him the benefit of the doubt.

He looked over at me, "Oh yeah? I'm sorry, ladies, I guess I'm kind of bad at reading through my emails. I get so much junk sent to me, I probably deleted it by mistake," he said in a rich baritone.

"It's no problem," Maya responded. *Yeah, she's gone.* I saw how Darren and Maya were eyeing one another.

"Well, it's nice to meet you, Darren," I said, extending my hand. That was followed by Maya extending her hand to him as well. He held on to her hand for a few seconds too long for a simple business handshake. By this point, the three of us were awkwardly standing in the front of the shop. "Would you like to give us a tour of your shop? Talk a little?" I asked to get us from in front of the door.

"Yeah, okay. I have an appointment coming in about ten minutes. Does that work for you ladies?" he asked.

"Yes," Maya answered. "We won't take up too much of your time."

"Okay, then, follow me." Darren took a little time to tell us how he was inspired to open his shop and all of the services offered to male and female clients. He wanted to have a place where men could be pampered, too, which explained why his skin looked like dark chocolate silk. Anyway, he led us toward the back of the shop, where there was a VIP room for clients who wanted a little more privacy while being serviced. There was a small unfinished space that was going to serve as a manicure and pedicure area. I thought that was a great addition to the shop. I noticed how Darren and Maya kept stealing looks and smiles at one another. I wanted to give them a little space to do or talk about whatever they wanted to, so I asked Darren, "May I use your restroom, please?"

"Yeah, sure, it's down the hall to the left," he answered.

I didn't need to do anything while I was in there, so I just pulled out my phone to see if I had any notifications. I had a text from Julian.

Julian: *Hey beautiful, are we still on for tonight?*

I smiled. Julian and I had been talking and flirting for the past few weeks. Today was the first time we were going on a date. I liked getting to know him, but I liked to take things slow, too. He seemed to be okay with that.

Me: *Yes. I'll be ready.*

I washed my hands and headed out of the restroom. I followed Maya and Darren's laughter from down the hall. I figured Darren's appointment must have been there by now. Maya and I needed to go look at the vacant rental space anyway.

When I got to the VIP room, Darren's client was in the chair, facing the mirror with his head down and eyes glued to his phone. I looked at Maya, who probably hadn't stopped smiling since we got there, and said, "Are you ready to check out the other space?"

She just looked at me and nodded toward the customer in the chair. I looked at her as if I were asking, *what*? She nodded again, and I gave her a confused look. Alerted by the sudden silence in the room, the client looked up in the mirror. That's when I saw his face in the reflection. There he sat, Wesley Johnson, Jr.

I gasped, and my mouth dropped open. Meeting him once was a treat; seeing him again had to be some type of sign, right? Both Maya and Darren laughed out loud at my reaction. Wesley stood up and placed his phone down in his chair. Turning to me, he said, "Miss Serenity James, it's nice to see you again. What are the odds?"

I smiled and stammered. "It's— It's nice to see you again, too." I looked over at Darren and Maya for answers.

"Renny, Wesley and Darren are best friends! Small world, right?"

"Right," I answered, now feeling like a ball of nerves.

I paused before I looked back to Wesley again. I felt his eyes on me. I could hardly make eye contact with him. However, in this setting, I could get an even better look at him than before. He was even finer than the first time I saw him, if that was even possible. His facial features were as close to perfect as a man could get, chocolate brown skin, chiseled jawline, full lips, almond-shaped eyes, and eyelashes that would make any woman jealous. His hair and beard had grown out a little more since the charity event, and it was a good look on him. Although his clothes were a little loose-fitting, I could see how muscular his chest and abs were. His arms and shoulders looked like he gave the most perfect hugs, too. He wasn't as big and muscular as Darren, but they probably worked out at the same gym. He had on an old-school style, all-black tracksuit with matching sneakers. His cologne smelled expensive; it intoxicated me on contact. I had always loved a good-smelling man. When I did make eye contact with him, his signature light gray   -blue eyes pierced right through me along with his million-dollar smile.

He took a few steps over to me with his arms open as if he were going to hug me. I let out a breath cause if I had held it in any longer, I would get dizzy. Meanwhile, Maya was over there standing with Darren, smiling like a Cheshire cat. He gave me a friendly hug that I didn't refuse. I was right, he did give the most perfect hugs. I secretly hoped some of his cologne would rub off on me too, I thought, as I breathed him in. I needed to calm down. I was making too big of a deal over him in my head.

"Well, I don't want to interrupt your appointment. Maya and I were just leaving," I said, sounding nervous and trying to exit the room with grace.

"You know, I didn't get a chance to ask you when we were at the charity event last month what your favorite Xtascy song is?"

I looked at Maya and Darren for some reason before answering, ""You Are," from the second album. That's my favorite.""

"Really?" he asked, with a nod of approval.

"Yes. That's my favorite. I keep that one on repeat when it plays." I blushed. He stared at me for a moment, making me shift my eyes from him.

"You've got good taste."

"Thank you."

Maya and Darren were engrossed in their own conversation when Wesley asked me, "Do you remember what you said to me that night at the charity event before you left?" He looked at me as if the thought had just hit him.

I remembered, but I didn't want to repeat it in front of Maya and Darren, so I just gave him a cautious, "Yes, I remember."

"Well, you were right," he admitted. We looked at each other for a long moment without words.

"Okay, Renny. You ready to go, girl?" Maya asked, and this time she was saving me from the handsome stranger who had captivated me.

"Yeah. Darren, it was nice to meet you. And Wesley, it was really good to see you again," I said, lingering a look on him before we exited the room.

Once we viewed the empty rental space, Maya and I retreated to her car, where she couldn't wait to talk about Darren and Wesley. "I gave him my number, so we'll see what happens," she said with excitement about Darren. "And what about you, smiling all in Wesley Johnson's face! *'You Are'* is my favorite song, I love you, I wanna have your babies, you are my life!" she teased, mocking my nervous behavior.

"Shut up!" I said, laughing at her accuracy.

"Here I am, a grown woman, and that man had me feeling like a little girl! I did not expect to see him in that room! I'm just glad he was nice about my weird behavior. I'm glad it wasn't worse," I said.

"You weren't acting weird. You were fine! Trust me!" Maya affirmed.

I knew Wesley lived somewhere in the outskirts of Charlotte. I had just never been in a circle of people where I would actually meet him once, let alone twice. "When thee Wesley Johnson walked into that room, I was surprised as hell, too! But I was trying to see what Darren was talking about! So, I played it cool!" Maya joked. "But, girl, I think he likes you!" she teased.

"Wesley?" I sucked my teeth and said, "Maya, come on now. No! That man does not like me! He was just being nice to a fan, and I appreciate that."

"Nice to a fan, huh? I'm a fan, and he didn't hug me like he hugged you! And he didn't look at me the way he was looking at you. He was eating you up with his eyes! Girl, you have to pay attention!" Maya's words had me blushing. "And what did he mean when he asked you about what you said to him at the charity event? What happened?"

I sighed, "Well, I told you he apologized for what Candice said about us being *the help*." Maya rolled her eyes.

"Yeah, that knock-off Beyoncé is lucky I was conducting business, or I would have handled her," she said without delay.

"Well, I didn't tell you that I told him that she wasn't a good person, and he could do better."

Maya's eyes almost jumped out of her head. "You told him that! Girl! What did he say?"

"Nothing. I pretty much left after I said it. I mean, the girl was screwing somebody in a closet and then stood next to him like nothing happened!" Maya obviously couldn't believe my boldness from the look on her face.

"Then they broke up like the next day?" Maya asked, feverishly scrolling through her phone to find the post about their breakup. "Well, that doesn't matter anyway," Maya continued, "You should go back in there and see what he says to you."

If "I'm crazy as hell" were a person, it would be Maya right now after that suggestion. It had only been maybe twenty minutes since we had left the barbershop, so he probably was still in there. I looked over at the storefront. "Go back in there and say what?" I asked, with my face scrunched up.

"Go give Darren your business card or something. I know he makes you a little nervous, but he's just a regular guy. And if he likes you, he'll make it obvious if you go back in there. But I can already tell he likes you! What do you have to lose?"

"My pride!" I shouted. "My dignity! Maya, I don't want to look like another groupie who just has to be around him. He's not interested in someone normal like me. He dates supermodels and women in the entertainment industry. I'll pass on that." With that being said, Maya knew she wouldn't convince me to change my mind.

Chapter Six

Wesley.

After picking up my phone, I sat back down in the barber's chair. D stood in the reflection of the mirror behind me with a smirk on his face. "What man?" I asked.

"Nothing, bro," D answered, holding his hands up in surrender. He grabbed the barber's cape, placed it around my neck, and looked at me again through the mirror. "Go ahead and ask, man," D said.

"Ask what?" I replied, confused.

"Okay, it's nothing. You good?"

"Yeah, I'm good," I answered with reassurance. D started to inspect my hair and beard then reached for his clippers. As soon as he turned them on, I asked, "So how do you know that Serenity girl and her friend? I mean, how did they end up in your shop of all places?"

D, unable to control his laughter, turned off the clippers, and said "I knew it, man! I know you! You can't fool me! They were fine, right?"

"Hell yeah, they were fine! They were at the charity dinner last month, and I met them that night. They were the caterers, but they didn't look like that!" I said, with a mental picture of them in my mind.

"I definitely didn't see them that night because I know I would have remembered them!" D said.

"I know you were feelin' shorty in the blue, but that Serenity girl, damn! Did you see her, man? She's gorgeous!" I said as we slapped each other's hands like teenage boys. "She has a good energy about her. You know, usually, when I ask a woman what their favorite Xtascy song is, they say "Georgia Peach." Nine times out of ten, that lets me know right there what they're trying to get into. Which I have no problem with!"

"Right, right," D interjected, turning his clippers back on.

I continued, "I can tell she's different, but in a good way."

"Yeah, I see what you mean, but I'm surprised, she's not your usual type," D said, picking out my hair.

"My *usual* type?" I asked, looking at him through the mirror.

"Yeah! Your *usual* type! You like those outspoken, aggressive, high maintenance, down for whatever type of chicks! Their bodies be thick, too! I'm surprised Mr. R&B didn't pop up and start trying to sing that girl right out of her clothes! That's the way you were looking at her, man. I remember that's how you used to do it! That's how we ended up with the two finest girls in high school at senior prom when we were just freshmen! I thought you were going all in with that favorite song line!"

We shared a laugh. The favorite song pick-up line had been my icebreaker for a long time, but it never steered me wrong when it came to determining what type of woman I had in front of me. "But for real, D. I ain't on that young boy stuff no more. I've had enough fun singing to women for their attention. I'm good on that! It's something about her that stopped me in my tracks. I knew I couldn't throw my usual game at her." D began shaping my hair up.

"You know she said something interesting to me that night at the mixer that I can't get out of my head," I said, trying to sound casual.

"She did? What did she say?"

"She told me that Candice wasn't a good person. That she didn't deserve me, and I could do much better."

D turned off the clippers and moved to stand in front of me. "Dawg! She said that to you?"

"Yup. I was so shocked when she said it that I didn't even say anything back. She's bold, just in a different type of way," I said.

Turning the clippers back on, D said, "She picked up on Candice's vibe after knowing her only five minutes? Yeah, I like her already!"

"There's something that I'm drawn to about her. I don't know what it is, but I want to see her again."

D explained to me who Serenity and Amaya were and why they were in the shop. I was impressed that they were the landlords of the property. We knew Amaya owned a catering company, but we weren't sure if Serenity was part owner or just worked for her. Either way, they seemed to have their business affairs in order. He said he planned on hitting up Amaya later today to see if she wanted to get a drink tonight. One thing about D, if he wanted something, he went all in for it. I, on the other hand, usually didn't react so fast. I liked to let things marinate for a minute before I decided what to do. I tried not to act on impulse, but Serenity kept flashing in my mind every time I had a dormant thought.

Though I played it cool when I laid my eyes on her, I was shook by how beautiful she was. The first time I met her, I thought she was cute, but I could take her all in today. She stood about five-four, and her soft brown golden skin looked like she nurtured a special relationship with the sun. Her long, natural hair was like in a wavy pattern, and it flowed down her back. She had dark chestnut-colored eyes, and her smile warmed the inside of my chest. She didn't have on heavy makeup; her DNA had her covered. She was slim and petite, which was a far departure from the type I usually went for. However, the way her sundress laid on her told me all I needed to know. Her whole look was a vibe. When I hugged her, she smelled like sweet, warm vanilla. Damn, I even noticed the nude-colored nail polish on her fingers and toes! Her physical beauty was obvious, though. She seemed like she had a warm and kind spirit, too. Yeah, I was definitely going to have to see her again.

After D finished me up, I opened my money app and sent him his payment, plus tip, of course. I checked myself out in the mirror and said, "Man, I don't know what I would do without you! This looks good, my G!"

"You know I got you, bro!" he said, brushing off my shoulders.

"Alright, man. I'll hit you later," I said, walking toward the door."

"You know, I can ask Amaya about her little homegirl if you want," he said, stopping my feet from moving forward.

I thought about it for a second. "Nah, man. I'm good," I responded, now unsure if I wanted to take it there.

"Look, I know you're into her. I can find out if she's at least single."

I nodded and said, "Alright, let me know."

Chapter Seven

Serenity.

I made it home with enough time to freshen up and change my clothes for my date with Julian. He said I could dress down in jeans if I wanted to because the place we were going to was pretty laid back. So, I changed into black denim skinny jeans and an off-the-shoulder yellow cream-colored top. I wore the same sandals from earlier, big hoop earrings, and since my hair was holding up from my twistout earlier, I just left it alone.

I agreed to let Julian pick me up at home. He said I should expect him at 7:00 p.m. I was comfortable letting him know where I lived since I didn't consider him a stranger. I was writing in my journal and listening to music when I heard my doorbell ring. I looked at the time to see it was almost seven o'clock. Julian was a little early. Before answering the door, I turned off my music and closed my journal. I opened the door to a casually dressed, handsome, and smiling Julian holding a bouquet of rainbow-colored roses. "Hi Julian," I greeted him with a sweet smile.

"Hi," he returned, stepping into the foyer. "I didn't know your favorite flower, so I didn't think I could go wrong with roses. I hope you like them," he said, giving me a warm hug and offering the flowers to me.

"They're beautiful. Thank you," I said. "Well, you're a few minutes early, so come in for a minute so I can put these in water and grab my shoes."

"Are you sure?" he asked, looking around inside.

"Yeah, come on in." I closed the door behind him as he stood in the foyer. Sensing he was a little hesitant to come in, I said, "I'll be right back. You can wait here."

I put the flowers in water. Then I slipped my shoes on, grabbed my purse, keys, sunglasses, and phone. As I walked back to the foyer to meet Julian, I saw I had a message on Instagram. Not wanting to be rude, I put my phone on vibrate and slipped it into my purse before my eyes met Julian's again. He gave me a searing stare, "You always look good at work, Serenity. But tonight, you look extra good with this whole casual look. I like it."

I blushed. "Thank you. You look handsome, too." I guess I never noticed how attractive Julian was before now. I mean, I had always seen him in his uniform, but I never wondered what he would look like without it. *Has he always been this fine?*

He was about six-one, athletically built with broad shoulders and caramel-colored skin. He wore his jet-black hair cut low and had waves for days. He donned a thin mustache and a neatly groomed beard. I noticed he wore diamond studs in his pierced ears and a simple silver-tone watch. He was dressed casually in a navy Lacoste polo shirt, dark blue denim jeans, and a pair of blue Chuck Taylor's with white soles. His scent was clean and fresh; I don't think it was cologne, though. I'll admit, he had the whole pretty boy thing going, and I was okay with all of it!

We shared a few seconds of eye contact before he asked, "Are you ready?"

Checking my purse, I said, "Uh, yes. Let's go."

I had Julian step outside before me so I could set my security alarm. We walked to his car, and he opened the door for me. He had a nice mid-sized SUV. A Jeep, I believe. His door was already unlocked, so I didn't do the reach over thing. Once in the car, I asked him, "So, where are you taking me tonight?"

He looked at me and replied, "It's a surprise. I hope you don't mind me taking control of the night, do you?"

I shrugged and said, "It's your world," with a playful smile. He started the engine and looked over at me again. "You really do look good tonight," he said, giving me another glance from head to toe.

As we hit the main road, he turned the music up but kept it low enough for us to still hold a conversation. "What type of music do you like?" he asked.

I laughed. "My music tastes are all over the place. But right now, I'm in my throwback R&B phase. It's all I've been listening to lately." I felt the urge to tell him about my run-in with Wesley this morning, but decided talking about another man on our first date was not the move.

"Oh!" he said like he already knew. "You like them, baby, please, on my knees, don't you ever leave me type of songs, huh?" he teased.

I laughed again. "I do. I like romance, and I like music that makes me think of what love could feel like."

He had a look that suggested he was storing that information for later. "Well, what type of music do *you* like?" I asked.

"I like some R&B, too, but I'm more into conscious rap. You know, music with lyrics that carry a message and forces you to elevate how you see the world around you. Not these mumble-rappers all over the radio. Don't get me wrong, I like some of it for entertainment, and it gets me hyped in the gym. But I like for my mind to be fed, too, you know?"

His phone began to ring through the Bluetooth in his car, and the name on the screen read, "Momma."

I glanced over at him as it seemed like he was deciding whether or not he wanted to answer it. "If you need to answer it, that's okay," I said.

"Nah, I'll call her back. I just spoke to her right before I picked you up."

We drove for about thirty minutes, having casual conversations before we made it to our destination. We arrived at a worn-down-looking brick building with small windows and no signage indicating what was inside. It didn't look like a dangerous neighborhood, just a little rundown. A few people were congregating in front of the building, talking and leaning on parked cars. I looked over at Julian with slight concern. "Is this the place?"

Proudly smiling, he said, "Yeah, this is it. You ready?"

I nodded and assured myself that Julian wouldn't take me anywhere unsafe. After grabbing a notebook and putting on an all-black fitted baseball cap he took from the backseat, Julian walked over to the passenger side door. He held his hand out to help me out of the car and closed the door. Once I got my footing, he must have read the look of concern on my face because he gave me an unexpected full contact hug that instantly warmed me. He lifted his baseball cap a bit, kissed me on the top of my head, and said, "It'll be okay as long as you're with me. I got you." He lowered his arms to offer me his free hand to hold as we walked across the street. I didn't object. I liked the care he took with me. He made me feel safe.

Approaching the building, I heard what sounded like someone talking on a microphone and low applause. When we entered, the man at the door greeted Julian, "Jay! Brotha! What's going on, man?"

"Nothing much, man. Hey, this is my friend, Serenity."

The gentleman gave Julian a look of approval, then he turned to me and said, "Nice to meet you. You going up there tonight?"

I looked confused and was about to speak when Julian replied, "Nah, man, this is her first time here. She's just here to support, you know."

The man nodded and said, "You want me to put you down?"

"Yeah, go ahead and do that," Julian responded.

After he paid the cover fee, we walked deeper into the small space to find a seat. "An open mic? You brought me to an open mic?" I asked, barely holding back my excitement.

"Yeah, I was kind of hoping you would like it. Are you happy with my surprise?" he asked, needing reassurance.

"I am. I've always wanted to come to one of these! I didn't take you for the poet type! Thank you!" I said, giving him a quick hug and scouting out a table to sit at. The venue didn't have good lighting; it was pretty dark in there. But the performance area did have a spotlight, so everyone could see the artist performing.

While the emcee was introducing the next talent, Julian explained that the venue, *Words & Verses,* offered a small menu if I wanted to order something to eat. I opted for some wings, fries, and a soda because I was getting hungry. Julian and I shared the food, and some insight, while listening to all of the acts that went up. Everyone was so talented and brave. I didn't think I could ever go up there and do that.

I genuinely enjoyed myself, and Julian introduced me to many people who stopped by the table to speak to him. We were sharing a laugh when a woman's voice came from behind us.

"Julian? Julian? Is that you?" she asked. The woman approached the table until she was in our line of view, which happened to be directly blocking the person performing. *Okay.*

"Hey, Carla," Julian said as if it hurt his lips to part with the salutation.

The woman glared at me before turning her attention back to Julian, "I see you out here looking good tonight, like always," the woman boldly said. I raised my eyebrows and looked over to Julian with a "what in the hell" facial expression. Julian visibly became irritated by the woman's presence and comments.

He popped up, looked down at me, and said, "Excuse me for a minute." He turned to Carla and said, "Let me talk to you for real quick."

I turned to watch as the woman followed him toward the front entrance. He appeared to be talking to her very firmly. The woman stood there with her arms folded, looking at him like she didn't care what he had to say, shaking her head and rolling her eyes at him. I saw him point over to our table while talking to her, which made me snap back around like a kid caught with my hand in the cookie jar. A minute or so later, he came back to the table and sat down with a heavy sigh. "I'm sorry about that," he whispered. "I'll explain that mess later."

I rubbed his back because he looked like he was a little stressed. I broke his mood by saying in his ear, "I'm really having a good time with you tonight. I'm glad we are here together." When I pulled back, he gifted me with a smile that ignited my heart. He grabbed my hand and kissed the back of it.

Our attention was pulled from one another when the emcee announced with excitement, "The next artist we have coming up is a longtime favorite of Words & Verses. Every time this brotha comes up here, he lights the microphone on fire! Y'all put your hands together for the Adonis Poet— Julian!" The small crowd applauded for Julian. He picked up his notebook that had been on the floor under his chair and made quick eye contact with me before walking up to the microphone. He shoulder bumped the host before adjusting the mic stand. "How y'all feeling tonight, good?" he asked.

Several people in the crowd responded with things like, "We alright if you're alright" and "We good."

He smiled, pushed his hat low to his eyes, and said, "I got one piece to do for y'all tonight." This was met with some groans of displeasure from the crowd. "I know, I know, but it's a good one! He looked over at me and said, "It's called *Serenity*."

I sank into my chair as everyone looked my way. I gave him a semi-smile, trying to act as if I wasn't scared to death of what he might say. He cleared his throat. The room quieted down:
I wish I could touch the hands of the God who made you,
Let me be clear, He made me, too.
But when He made you,
It must have been the day He figured out that certain beauty can't be described,
Just experienced.
He wasn't stingy or selfish or prideful when it came to your beauty.

He gave without reservations,
Without hesitations,
And now we all get to bask in his proclamations through you.
I wish I could touch the hands of the God who made you.
Because when He made you,
He made sure your beauty was more than skin deep.

He made sure your beauty rivaled the morning sunrise, a perfect rainstorm, the stars among the clouds.
He made your beauty quiet,
But resoundingly loud.
And when He made your heart, is when He became most proud.
I wish I could touch the hands of the God who made you.
Because I just want to shake His hands.
I want to thank Him for designing and executing His grandest of plans… through you.
I want to thank Him for setting you free, so I could have the chance to experience you every time you're looking at me.
I never want you to stop looking at me.
And, I just wish I could touch the hands of the God who made you.

He raised his hat to reveal his eyes and looked at me. Then he delivered the final word of the poem, "Serenity."

The crowd erupted! Everyone was on their feet applauding him. The crowd was so loud that I barely heard him say into the microphone, "Thank you, Words & Verses." He left the performance area and was bombarded with compliments and pats on the back. I sat there, not knowing how to respond. *Did he really say he wanted to shake God's hand for making me?*

I was overwhelmed, flattered, and flustered all at the same time. I had to get some air. I got up from my seat, snatched my purse, and went outside to take some deep breaths. This was all a little too much for me. There was a small group of people outside the door holding court, completely oblivious to what had just taken place.

A minute or so after I exited the building, Julian came outside looking worried. "Serenity, are you alright?" he asked.

I couldn't even look at him. I had a mixture of nerves and embarrassment coursing through me. "Yeah," I said, exhaling and looking at him. "I just needed some air."

"I guess you didn't like the poem?" he asked, sounding disappointed.

"Julian, it was a nice poem. Beautiful, actually, but we've only been getting to know each other for a short while, and that was a lot for me."

He looked defeated. "Julian, I—"

"November ninth," he interrupted me.

"What?" I was confused.

"November ninth was the first time I saw you. I think my heart skipped a beat the first time you looked at me. I didn't know you, but I knew I wanted to. It took me this long to even ask you out on a date. I didn't mean to make you feel uncomfortable. I'm sorry. I know it's only been a few weeks for you, but it's been months for me and I—" he sighed. "I just wanted to let you know how special I think you are. You're smart, successful, kind, and the most beautiful woman I've ever seen. I can tone it down and take it slow because I know that's what you want, but this is just how I am." Before I knew it, he pressed his lips against mine for the softest, sweetest, most passionate kiss I can ever remember having.

I released his lips, took a step back, and looked up at his eyes. I was speechless and a bit woozy. He looked down at me with desire mounting behind his gaze. "Maybe you should take me home now," I whispered.

He advanced even closer toward me and placed his arms around my waist, giving me a chance to resist his next move. Then, he laid a kiss on me that was so electric I felt like I was hit by lightning. *What is this? How did we go from A to Z in two seconds flat?* But, damn! He knew how to kiss, though. I know he wanted to do more, evidenced by his fingertips firmly digging into the exposed skin of my back. However, he remained a gentleman by keeping his hands in place. Our kiss ended with us looking at one another. I felt like I was transported to a different planet! "I do need to get you home," he said, using a low tone, releasing his grip on me.

He held my hand and walked me across the street to the passenger side of his car, closing the door behind me once I was tucked inside. We rode without words. Just the music was playing. Half of an hour later, we were pulling up in my driveway. He put the car in park and cut off the engine. "Julian, I really enjoyed my time with you tonight. Thank you." I said, breaking our silence.

"Me too," he responded. "I hope I didn't scare you off tonight with the poem and the kiss. It's just how I express myself."

I kept my eyes on him. "If it's okay with you, I would like to see you again, Serenity. Next time, you can choose the place," he said, flashing me his pearly whites.

I returned his smile. "That would be nice."

"Let me walk you to your door," he said, unbuckling his seatbelt. He escorted me to my front door and stood behind me on the steps below. Before I put my key in the door, I turned to him and said, "Good night, Julian."

"Good night, Serenity James."

I turned and unlocked my door, gave him a quick wave, and said, "Text me when you get home." He nodded. I pushed open my door and closed it. A few moments later, I heard him drive away.

Julian was my first date in close to two years. It's not that I hadn't been approached before now, I just wanted to make sure I was ready to date again before saying yes to someone. It was 11:30 p.m. when I heard my phone buzzing in my purse. I realized I hadn't checked my phone all night while I was with Julian, and that rarely happens to me. I had already showered, pinned up my hair, and gave myself a clay mask facial before snuggling up in my bed to write in my journal. I saw I had four text messages. One was from Julian, and three were from Maya:
Julian: *I made it home. I'll call you tomorrow. Sleep well, beautiful.*

Me: *Ok. Thank you again for tonight! Ttyl.*
Then there were Maya's messages:
Maya: *I'm out with Darren at the Ale House. Girl, he's even finer at night! (8:02 pm).*
Maya: *Renny, girl, I need to talk to you! I got some tea! (9:32 pm).*
Maya: *Girl, if you get this before 11:30, call me! We need to talk! (11:12 pm).*

As much as I wanted to talk to Maya, I figured I'd wait until the morning. I'd had a long day and was worn out. The last thing I checked was the message from Instagram I had ignored earlier. When I scrolled through my DM's and saw his name, @WesleyfromXtascy, my heart dropped down into my stomach. I nervously tapped on the message to open it, and couldn't believe what I was reading:

Miss Serenity James, it was nice seeing you again today. If it's okay with you, I would like the opportunity to see you again if you're free next weekend.

I had to read the message at least ten times before I believed it came from him. He wanted to take me out on a date? I was floored and didn't know how to respond to him. For now, I would just sleep on it.

Chapter Eight

Wesley.

After leaving the barbershop, I decided to ride around the city for a bit because it was such perfect weather. I called up my cousin, Jackie, to see if she was available to have lunch with me. She didn't live too far from downtown; plus, I hadn't seen her in a while. She met me at a little diner called Pete's. I got there first and stood to hug her when she arrived. "Hey, cousin!" she greeted me with a happy smile. "You look good," she said as we sat down.

"Thanks, you look good, too. How have you been?" I asked, just as the waitress came over with two glasses of ice water.

"Do you two need a few minutes to order?" she asked.

"Yes, please," Jackie responded, settling herself in the chair.

"Okay, I'll be back in a few minutes," the waitress said, giving me a lingering look before walking away.

Jackie looked at me, "You and Uncle Wes just can't help yourselves!"

I laughed. "Jackie, I'm literally just sitting here!" I said, holding my hands up.

"Uhm hmm…" she responded. "Anyway, cousin, I'm doing well. Really well, actually. You know, I'm finally going back to school for my Master of Psychology degree!" she said.

"Oh yeah? I've been telling you that you need to go ahead and finish up school. You've been analyzing folks since we were kids! *Wesley Junior, it's okay for boys to cry if they're hurt. Don't be ashamed to get it out*," I teased, imitating her as a child and taking a sip of water.

She almost fell out of her chair from laughter. "Yeah! That was me! And I was right, too! But I've put off finishing school long enough. I feel ready now."

"Good," I said as if I were her mentor.

"What's new with you, cousin? I saw that you and Candice broke up. Everybody was talking about it. Are you okay?"

I lowered my eyes to my phone. "Yeah, I'm good. She just turned out to be someone I obviously didn't know. I haven't talked to her since it happened; don't plan on it either," I declared. "Anyway, how's Uncle Bobby doing?" I asked, changing the subject.

The waitress returned to take our orders and stalled at the table a little longer than needed. Jackie read the look on the young woman's face and politely asked, "Would you like to take a picture with him, darling?"

I didn't ever want to assume that anyone knew who I was, especially since it had been a long while since I'd been on TV regularly. The young woman gave Jackie a pleasant smile, "Yes!" she answered, turning to me. "If you don't mind?"

"I don't mind at all," I answered.

After we ate, we had a good conversation reminiscing about old times. "Jackie, let me get your opinion on something," I said.

"I met someone …"

"Oh, Lord!" Jackie shouted.

I laughed. "It's not like that! Listen, I met someone, and I can't stop thinking about her."

"Okay, so what's the problem?"

"I don't know how to approach her. I'm used to dealing with women in the industry, and most of the time, they end up approaching me!" I chuckled. "But this girl is different. She's smart and kind, and I don't know if being *Wesley from Xtascy* makes much of a difference to her."

"First and foremost, it's not like you were in some unknown group that had one hit. Y'all had multiple hits and sold-out arenas! That's a huge deal!" Jackie said.

"I know. But you know, I'm not the look at me type," I replied. "I don't want her to see me as that. I want her to get to know the man behind all of that."

"Well, cousin, it is a big part of who you are, and that's what people will expect of you. You've always been humble and gracious. But you've worked hard for your success, and I don't think you should downplay your achievements to make someone else feel comfortable. You've never been the type to make others aware of your presence. Still, you need to be a whole person, and whoever you're with needs to see you being who you are, not the version of you that you think they want. That's how you'll know who really cares about you or who's just around to be around. As far as this new woman you're talking about, you just need to be honest. Women respond to that. If you want to take her out, tell her. If you think she's beautiful, say it. You're a good guy with so many exceptional qualities. Being yourself is all you need to do, and if she doesn't respond to that, then it's on to the next!"

Jackie's advice hit me hard and no doubt gave me much to think about. We caught up a bit more before leaving the diner. Catching up with her was just what I needed. Ever since my breakup with Candice, I hadn't felt much like seeing anyone. After seeing Serenity today, Candice was the furthest thing from my mind. On my drive home, I thought about what Serenity had said about the song she liked, "You Are," and I decided to play it. I hadn't heard it in a while, and as soon as I heard the first notes, it felt like I was visiting an old friend. As it played, I imagined I was singing it to Serenity. I pictured that sweet smile forming across her beautiful face. Her energy was so magnetic.

I pulled up to my house close to 6:00 p.m. It had been a long day. I found myself getting comfortable on the couch when I pulled up Instagram on my phone. I felt a little out of place doing it, but I looked up Serenity to see if she had a profile. Her profile picture showed her smiling face, and she had on a flower headband with all of her pretty hair on display. I clicked on her profile picture to see what else I could learn about her. There was not much info in her profile, except that she earned her MBA from the University of North Carolina, Charlotte, and worked in finance, but it didn't say where.

Her feed mostly consisted of selfies, motivational quotes, throwback pictures, and many snaps of her friend, Amaya, acting silly. *No boyfriends, though.* Her page was modest, and I liked the fact that she showcased being comfortable in her own skin but not over the top. I kept scrolling on her feed until I found I had gone back a couple of years. So, I called it what it was: stalking. I was officially stalking her page. I could admit to that, as embarrassed as I felt about it. I had gathered snacks and everything. I saw a post that was a short video. It was dated two years prior. My curiosity made me tap it open. I had already fallen into the rabbit hole by then. It was a thirty-second clip of her and Amaya dancing to trap music! I laughed out loud at that post. I couldn't ignore how happy she looked when she danced. I could hear people in the background of the video laughing and egging them on. She seemed like she was just as fun as she was beautiful and smart.

Jackie's advice of just taking the honest approach with Serenity played back in my head. I hadn't heard back from D on whether or not he found out if she was single, so I decided to just shoot my shot, anyway. I figured if she weren't interested, she would let me know. I contemplated what to say before settling on the simple route:

Miss Serenity, it was nice seeing you again today. If it's okay with you, I would like the opportunity to see you again if you're free next weekend.

Then I hit send. The ball was now officially in her court.

Chapter Nine

Serenity.

I usually allowed myself to sleep in a little more on Sunday mornings, just because I could. I woke up thinking about yesterday's events, my date with Julian, running into Wesley again, and him asking me out on a date. So much had happened in such a short span. I grabbed my phone and went back to the message Wesley sent me last night. Looking at it made me feel like I was in a dream. *He wants to see me again?* I snickered. I felt a mix of emotions about it, but I knew I had to respond to him one way or another. He was the type of man women fantasized about, not dated. I was mulling over how I would respond to Wesley when I got a text from Julian:

Julian: *Good morning beautiful. I hope you slept well.*
Me: *Morning. I did. I'm just waking up.*
Julian: *Good. I know it's short notice, but would you like to have brunch with me today?*
Me: *That sounds good, but I can't today. I have some things I need to do at home. Raincheck?*
Julian: *Ok, cool. Can I call you later?*
Me: *Sure.*

Getting that text from Julian snapped me into reality about living in a dream world with Wesley. Julian and I weren't exclusive and had just been on one date. I did like what I knew of him, and we were still just getting to know one another. *Would it even be okay if I decided to see Wesley, too?* I'd never really dated more than one man at a time; it just wasn't my thing. But were Julian and I dating? Or did we just go out on one date? Then I thought about the poem he wrote me and those kisses he put on me less than twenty-four hours ago. I melted down into my bed at the thought of it. I took a heavy sigh and figured I didn't need to have all of the answers right then and there. It was too much to think about first thing in the morning.

After getting up and having my coffee, I gave Maya a call. I knew she went out with Darren last night, and I was sure she couldn't wait to fill me in on how it went. It was almost noon when a grouchy Maya answered the phone, "Hey, Renny," Maya said in a voice that sounded like she hadn't slept since I last saw her.

"Maya, are you okay? What time did you get in last night?" I asked, concerned.

Maya let out a sleepy sigh before answering, "Girl, I ain't get to bed until like 5:30 in the morning. After Darren and I left the Ale House, we went over to the club and stayed until it closed. After that, we went to the Waffle House. When we left, he followed me home. We sat up and talked until I fell asleep on the couch."

"Girl, you let that man in your house?" I asked in disbelief. "I know he's cute and all, but you don't even know him like that."

"I know, Renny, I know. I just felt like it would be okay at that moment because we were having such a good time."

"Maya, you have to be more careful than that."

"I know, but Darren was cool. He must have put me in the bed before he left because I woke up a few hours ago in bed all tucked in."

"You weren't drinking, were you?"

"No. I just had one drink at the bar, and I drank water the rest of the night. I'm just tired."

"As long as you're okay, I'm okay."

"Yeah, I'm good. I really like him, Renny. I mean, really, really like him."

We talked more about her night with Darren and my night with Julian, specifically about the poem he wrote for me. I didn't have a chance to tell her about the message I got from Wesley because she interrupted me with a "Girl!" that held a surge of energy she hadn't possessed seconds earlier. "Guess who wants to know if you're single?"

I paused and asked, "Who?"

"Wesley Johnson, girl! That's why I was texting you last night! After we left the barbershop, Wesley asked Darren to see if you were single!"

"What?!"

"Well, he didn't ask me directly; he tried to be casual with it. But, anyway, I told you he likes you! I saw the look on his face!"

My smile grew a mile long. "What else did he say?" I asked, wanting to know more of the tea.

"He ain't tell me anything else, and I didn't want to push the issue. But as soon as he went into the men's room I texted you. Apparently, Darren and Wesley have been friends since they were thirteen years old."

"Well, what did you tell him?"

"What do you think I told him? I said that you're single because you are! Going on one date with Julian does not make you his girlfriend."

"That's true, but—"

"I'm not going to let you talk yourself out of seeing Wesley because I know you want to! It's okay to have options. You're not married; you're not in a committed relationship, so there's no need to feel guilty," Maya interrupted.

"Maya," I called out to her, stopping her rant. "Wesley messaged me last night on Instagram asking me out on a date next weekend," I spilled.

"What?! Why didn't you tell me?" Maya shrieked.

"I didn't have a chance to. We were talking about Darren and Julian and …"

"Renny, that should have been the first thing you said!"

"So, did you answer him?"

"Not yet. I need to think about it first."

"I know I can't tell you what to do, but I think you should go. You used to yearn after this man, and now you have the chance to actually get to know him! If nothing else, you'll be able to say you went out on a date with your celebrity crush!"

"Yeah, that's true. I just don't know what he would want from me. You saw his ex, Candice; she's gorgeous."

"You are gorgeous, too," Maya rebutted. "She's pretty, but she had a terrible attitude, and she was cheating on Wesley with his friend in a public place! Don't sell yourself short. Ever. You are the prize, and he knows it. Shoot! Julian knows it, too, talking about how he wants to shake God's hand and all of that stuff!" I burst out in laughter at Maya's comment.

"And plus, you don't even know who that Carla woman is that was all in his face last night. Girl, you better message Wesley back and say I do!"

"I do?" I questioned.

"Yes," Maya continued, "*I do* want to go out with you; *I do* think you are fine as hell; *I do* want to cook you breakfast in bed; I *do* want to birth all your little gray-eyed babies! I do!" We both laughed into the phone at Maya being Maya. She did have some valid points, though. Wesley did seek me out, and I didn't know who that woman Carla was to Julian. I figured as long as I was going to be honest about it, I couldn't find a reason why I couldn't date them both. So, that's what I decided to do.

Maya and I had discussed finding a new tenant for our property, so I emailed a few leads as well. Once I handled my business, I sent Wesley a message confirming that I was available to see him next weekend. I also sent him my phone number and address, which he requested quickly after my response. I didn't know what to expect, but I was excited at the thought of what we might do. I had another message waiting for me from @InfinityRecVP. Without thinking, I opened the message, and it read:

Serenity, I'm having a private party next weekend, and I want you to be my special guest. You can bring a friend. Hit me back. Sean.

He left an address and the time I should arrive. I couldn't believe he was messaging me after I saw him almost ready to impregnate Candice in a random broom closet at that event last month. I didn't like this guy, and his message turned my stomach. I deleted the message and blocked him. Hopefully, I wouldn't have to deal with him again.

Sunday afternoons usually consisted of me washing my hair and going over financial paperwork in my home office while deep conditioning my well-trained tresses. I did laundry and some light cleaning before ordering my groceries to be delivered. It was early afternoon when I decided to take a short nap that I obviously needed. When I woke up, I laid out my clothes for work and went over the schedule of clients I would be meeting for the upcoming week. I had an invite to sit in on a meeting with Sharon and new high-profile clients on Wednesday. This wasn't an unusual request, but they didn't come too often.

Chapter Ten

Wesley.

It was a typical Sunday in my theater room when Serenity responded to my message on Instagram, agreeing to see me next weekend. I was watching "Pulp Fiction," one of my favorite Quentin Tarantino movies when I got the alert. I was filled with anxiety when I opened her response, hoping she agreed. This was a foreign feeling to me, I had never had a woman turn me down for anything, honestly, and the thought of her saying no made me nervous. I was in uncharted territory. I was a confident man when it came to women, but I realized it had been based on not ever having to work for a woman's affection. I felt Serenity was different, and I didn't want to mess up the chance to get to know her.

So, I officially had about a week to plan a date with Serenity. Honestly, I had no clue where to start! I knew my normal hang-out spots wouldn't work. Besides, I wanted to do something other than dinner and a movie. So, I had to think outside the box. I hit up D to see if he could come through and chat with me for a minute. His barbershop was closed on Mondays, so I figured he wouldn't mind coming over if he wasn't busy. He got to my house around nine o'clock with some new exotic beers he wanted me to try. D had an affinity for trying different types of beers. He was like a beer aficionado. Some of his selections had been pretty good, though.

We went back to my theater room, where I had restarted my movie. "Man, you never told me last night if Serenity is single, so I just hit her up anyway," I stated.

"Oh, word? My bad, man. Amaya and I were vibing heavy last night. She told me Serenity is single, but it slipped my mind to let you know. We were out until four or five o'clock this morning."

"What? Was y'all *out* late, or was y'all *up* late?" I asked, giving him a knowing look.

D laughed, "Nah, bro, it wasn't even like that. We really were just kicking it all night. We hit the bar, the club, Waffle House, and then we spent the rest of the night at her place just talking."

"Just talking?" I asked, giving him a look of disbelief.

"Yeah, man. That's it. She fell asleep on the couch. I picked her up, laid her down in her bed, and left."

I scoffed. "You have definitely changed, man!" I said, shaking my head while taking a sip of beer.

"Naw, she's just different. She looks good, got her own business, and she has a good head on her shoulders. She has a lot going for her, bro."

"I have a week to come up with a date idea to impress Serenity," I said. I knew the effort I put into this date would make all of the difference in whether or not we continued to see one another. We bounced a few ideas off of each other, but nothing stood out. Though I didn't mind being seen in public, going out with a new woman so soon after my breakup with Candice would definitely attract attention. I didn't want Serenity to be a part of some gossip blog. It was around 11:30 at night when D left. We hadn't come up with any good ideas, but we did end up watching the rest of the movie.

Chapter Eleven

Serenity.

Some Monday mornings just hit *different*. I loved my job. But some Mondays, I just wanted to roll over in bed and go back to sleep, and today was one of those days. I'm disciplined when it comes to working, and I hardly ever took any days off that weren't scheduled in advance. But today, I thought I was going to do just that. I reached out to my boss and let him know I'd be taking a personal day and working remotely for a couple of hours this morning. I had three clients scheduled to come in, but I asked the appointment desk to reschedule them and call me if they had any trouble. My boss and I had a great rapport, so taking the day off was not a problem. I logged in, sent off a few documents, and responded to a few emails before I laid back down in the bed. This was nice.

It was 10:30 a.m. when my phone rang. I looked down to see Julian's name on the screen. I answered. "Hello? Serenity, are you okay?" he asked, sounding concerned.

I wasn't surprised by his call. After all, he did text me this morning, and I had yet to respond. Then I didn't show up for work, so I'm sure he was worried.

"Yeah, I'm just taking a personal day. Everything is alright."

"Okay," he said, sounding relieved. "When I didn't hear back from you this morning, I thought that something was wrong, then you didn't come in. I'm just glad you're okay."

"I'm sorry, I didn't mean to make you worry, but I'm good. I promise."

"Do you need me to bring you anything? I can come by on my lunch break."

I chuckled. "I'm good, Julian. I appreciate you calling. Will you call me later on?" He reluctantly agreed before we ended the conversation.

Sleep hit me for the second time, having me wake up at 1:00 p.m. I couldn't figure out why I was so tired all of the time lately. I didn't feel sick, just a little rundown. I thought it would be a good idea to see my doctor, just to make sure everything was okay. I scheduled myself for a physical for later on in the week. I read my short conversation with Wesley from last night over and over again. Then I got a text from an unknown number:

Unknown Number: *How are you?*
Me: *I'm good. Who is this?*

I saw bubbles appear then disappear. Then they appeared again. Then I received a picture of a cute little brown-skinned boy playing a piano, showing all of his teeth for the camera. The picture was obviously old, evidenced by the white tube socks with the blue stripes around the top. I laughed out loud. Instantly, I knew it was Wesley, and my heart raced. I saved his number.

Me: *OMG! You were so cute!*
Wesley: *LOL! Thank you. That's a picture from my private collection, so don't show anyone!*

Since he had shared a throwback with me, I decided to send him a picture of me on my first day of school.

Wesley: *Wow! Nice pic! So, I see you've always been that beautiful, huh?*

His message jolted my heart.
Me: *Thank you.*

Wesley: *How's your day going so far?*

Me: *It's fine. I'm home. I decided to take a personal day.*
Wesley: *You're not sick, are you?*
Me: *No, I just took an extra day.*
Wesley: *Okay. I just wanted to check in with you. I'm meeting up with my dad right now. Can I call you after?*

Just then, I remembered his dad, Wesley Johnson Sr., of the infamous singing group Midnight Stars, was a soul music legend! I don't know how that could have ever slipped my mind.

Me: *That's fine. Can you tell your dad that my mom is one of his biggest fans?*
Wesley: *I will. I'm sure he'll get a kick out of that!*

Having skipped breakfast altogether, I went to the kitchen to make a quick lunch and a cup of hot ginger tea. I wrote in my journal before falling back to sleep on the couch. My doorbell ringing awakened me. I woke up groggy and confused. I made my way to the front door, opening it after it rang for the second time. I didn't even look through my peephole; I just wanted to know who was at my house in the middle of the afternoon. A young, skinny man with a beautiful arrangement of flowers stood before me. "Are you Serenity James?" he asked.

Adjusting my eyes to the bright sun, I said, "Yes, that's me."

"I need you to sign here," he said, routinely placing a small screen in front of me. I signed my initials with one hand, and he handed me the flowers in the other. I thanked him and began to close the door when he said, "Oh, ma'am, I have one more. I can bring it in if you want."

More? "Okay, that's fine."
I waited by the door, holding the large arrangement

while he retrieved another one that was just as beautiful. I led him into the den, where we placed the flowers down. I thanked him and walked him to the door. I eagerly went back to the den to see who had sent me these flowers. I found the note in the arrangement I carried that read: *Beautiful flowers for a beautiful woman. See you this Saturday, Wesley.*

My heart warmed in my chest. I had a smile no one could pay me enough to get rid of. I looked at the other arrangement, and there was a note in that one, too. It read, *To Serenity's Mother, I'm glad you've enjoyed my music after all of these years. Stay beautiful, Wesley Sr.*

Get out of here! Not only did he send me flowers, but his dad sent flowers for my mom, too? *Wow.* He was already setting the tone for our date, and I liked it.

Making my way over to my bedroom, I held on to the notecard from the flowers. It was close to 3:00 p.m., and I hadn't showered yet. I was finding the perfect playlist to fit my mood when my phone rang. It was Wesley, and my heart stalled. I answered the phone using the sweetest and most flirtatious voice I could muster after all the sleeping I'd done today.

"Hello?" I answered.

"Hello, Serenity. How are you?" he asked.

"I'm good and thank you for the flowers! I love them! I haven't called my mom yet, but I'm sure she will tell me to thank your dad. This will make her day! I just hope my dad doesn't get too jealous," I laughed.

He sounded so smooth over the phone. His voice was deep, like he was getting ready to do one of those talking interludes on a love song.

"Yeah, well, I'm glad you like them." I could tell he was smiling just as hard as me.

"Well, I'll have to hold on to my mom's flowers because she lives in Virginia. I'll take a picture for her, though."

"Virginia? Oh, I'm sorry. I thought she lived locally. Is that where you're originally from?"

"Yup, born and raised in good ol' VA."

"Okay," he said, still projecting a smile through his voice. "So, what were you and your dad doing today? Talking about forming a father and son singing duo called Wes and Wes?"

"Oh, you got jokes? Okay!" He laughed, "My dad and I meet up a few times a month to check in with one another. I gotta make sure the old man is alright, you know?"

"Yeah, that's cool. Your dad is a whole living legend out here; that's amazing! He must have been very proud when you chose singing as your career."

"Yeah, he was. He was my mentor. So, how have you been spending your day off?"

"Believe it or not, I've just been resting. It feels nice and was much needed. But I'll be back to work tomorrow." The phone became silent for a few moments. "Where are you headed to now?" I asked.

"I volunteer at the Boys & Girls Club a few times a month. I help the kids with music. Some of them write songs, some play instruments, some sing—you know, stuff like that. That's where I'm headed now," he explained.

"That's wonderful! I love that you're sharing your gifts with the next generation of artists. I'm sure they're excited that *you* are their mentor."

Wesley laughed. "Well, not really. Most of them don't know who I am! Their parents do, though. One of the kids Googled me a while back, and now they've all seen my old videos on YouTube! They'll joke about my clothes and hairstyles from back then. But for the most part, they're not impressed!" We laughed at that. "Yeah, they keep me humble," he said. "But really, I learned a lot from my dad about being humble, gracious, and giving back. My dad has always been my best example of the type of man I want to be. Even at the height of his career, he always reminded me how important it is to give back to our community. He's a good man."

"I believe it. He raised you, and you seem like you're a good man, too. Not to mention the flowers he sent for my mom. I can tell your dad is a player from way back!" We laughed again. "Wesley, I'll admit I'm a little surprised a guy like you is showing any interest in someone like me." I needed to know if I was just another woman he was set out to conquer. I didn't want to be treated like a groupie or something.

"A guy like me? What do you mean?"

"Well, you're a well-known public figure. I'm sure you're recognized almost everywhere you go. Your dad is a legend. You've traveled the world, and I'm sure you've met many gorgeous women who are more … on your level," I said, not able to find a more appropriate way to say it. By no means had I thought I wasn't worthy of a man's interest. I knew I was a catch. I was just being realistic. There had never been a multi-millionaire vying for my attention.

He paused. "Serenity, yes, I do come from that world, but that's not who I am. I look to the heart of people. Whether or not they're famous or rich doesn't make a difference to me. I love singing and performing, but the celebrity part of it I could do without. I'm proud of my contribution to the music industry. But at the end of the day, it's business, and I did a job. Don't get me wrong; there are definite perks! I do get recognized a lot when I go out, but everyone is generally nice." He stopped himself from ranting on. "When it's all said and done, I really want you to look at me as a guy who is trying his best to impress a pretty girl."

There was a silence between us, then he said, "Serenity, you're not the average woman, and I saw that the night I met you. You looked me in my eyes and told me I deserved someone better than Candice. You didn't even know me personally, but you cared enough to say what you felt. You're the type of energy I want to be around. You're the type of woman I want to get to know. I'm glad that you're interested in a guy like me, honestly."

I was speechless for a few seconds. "Thank you for saying that, Wesley. It means a lot."

"You're welcome, and I genuinely mean it. Well, I've been sitting in this parking lot for about ten minutes now. I need to go inside. I just wanted to hear your voice and make sure you got the flowers. I'll text you later, okay?"

"Okay. Bye, Wesley." After he disconnected, I took a moment to absorb what he said about him wanting to be around my type of energy. I didn't think anyone had described me quite that way before. It felt…nice.

$$*****$$

I showered and dressed before calling my mom and telling her about Wesley and the flowers Wesley's dad had sent to her. When she recalled how popular Mr. Johnson's singing group was back in the day, she giggled and laughed with me like we were old girlfriends. We were on the phone for close to an hour, and we had a nice conversation. Before I knew it, it was five o'clock. I didn't feel like doing much more of anything but sinking in the bed. Julian texted me as soon as he got off from work and asked if he could stop by to check in on me. Knowing we needed to talk led me to agree to his visit.

He arrived in casual clothes. He hugged, and kissed me on my forehead as he stepped in. I didn't resist. It felt nice, but I felt guilty. My agreed-on date with Wesley popped into my mind.

"I'm glad to see you; I was worried about you," Julian said.

"I'm good, just a little tired. Come in; have a seat," I said. He followed me to the living room. We got comfortable on my couch. He took my hand and said, "I've been thinking about you all day."

Now I felt even guiltier. "Julian, there's something I need to ask you."

He sighed, "Is it about the woman from the other night? Carla? Listen, she and I had a little 'friends with benefits' situation going on. But once I started talking to you, I ended it."

I sat back and listened as he continued, "I want to be honest with you. I don't want to play any games. I know we're not exclusive, and we've only been out once. But I really like you, Serenity. I hope we can work toward becoming more than just friends," he confessed.

Welp, here it goes. "Thank you for clarifying who Carla is; she was really bold!" I chuckled, and then I sighed before saying, "Julian, my last relationship ended very badly. I don't want to get into the details of it, but it made me take a step back for a while to make sure I was okay before I even thought about dating someone new." He stared at me, "I want to be honest with you, too, Julian. I do like you, but like you said, we're not exclusive, and I—"

"You what?" he urged.

"I just want to make sure you know that I will still see other men from time to time. I'm just starting to date again. I don't think I'm ready to be tied down just yet, and I want to be upfront with you."

He loosened his grip on my hand and sat back against the couch. His eyes drifted toward me like he was trying to find the words to say, but he didn't say anything. I tried to hold up a neutral face, only having a conversation like this wasn't in my comfort zone. I had to be honest with him, though. Then, his reaction surprised even me. "Truthfully, I don't like the thought of you seeing someone else while you're seeing me. I don't even want to think about someone else hugging you, holding you, kissing you," he began, shaking his head. "But I understand. We're not together, and you're a beautiful woman. I was surprised that you were single to begin with because, well, you have so much to offer. But if this is what you want to do, I'm not going to try and stop you. Just know that I'm not interested in being second to another man. So, you do you, and I'm going to fall back and do me. You can come to me when you're ready because I want all of you," he said in a respectful manner. I sat at a loss for words. I didn't know what to expect, but that wasn't it.

I couldn't believe I was in my feelings over a man I'd only gone out with once. He saw the look of torment on my face and reached over to pull me onto his chest and held me. He stroked my hair and said, "It's okay, Serenity. Don't feel bad. It will all work out." He held me like that for a few minutes before saying he was heading out. I stood to walk him to the door, and he turned to give me one final hug.

When I pulled back from our hug, his eyes met mine, and he leaned over to kiss me. At first, it was just a quick kiss on my forehead, then on my nose, then on my lips. Then he came back to my lips for seconds, sliding his tongue into my mouth, kissing me like I was holding his next breath hostage. His arms wrapped around my waist, and he pulled me closer. I felt all of him pressed up against me. My body heat surged. I heard myself whimper or moan or something. He moaned a soft, "Mmmm," into my mouth as well. I felt the grip of his hands starting to lower from my waist. I released my lips from his. "Julian," I whispered, trying to catch my breath. "No."

He stared down at me, connecting his eyes with mine and taking inventory of the mess he had made of me. "I know," he whispered. "I just wanted to give you something to think about in the meantime." He wiped his bottom lip with his thumb and gave me a smirk. He pecked me on my cheek and said, "I'll see you tomorrow at work. Have a good night, beautiful." He opened the door and left.

Chapter Twelve

Wesley. Wednesday Morning.

Today, Dad and I had our first meeting with Trevor over at his new firm, Truest Financial. We drove separate vehicles because we were parting ways after our appointment. We arrived and were escorted up to the 6th floor by a security guard, a courtesy that wasn't necessary, but we thought was a nice touch. Once we got to Trevor's overly spacious office, we were greeted by him, and a woman named Sharon. "Serenity," I said in surprise. My heart skipped a beat. I hadn't initially seen her when I walked into the room. But I saw her now, and it made my early morning commute well worth it.

"Hi, Mr. Johnson and Mr. Johnson, nice to meet you," she greeted Dad and me, extending her hand to shake.

I understood she wanted to remain professional, but my whole professional demeanor stepped to the side for a moment. I had an overwhelming desire to grab her and hug her in front of everyone. I centered myself, though. "Oh, so you already know my clients?" Trevor asked Serenity.

"Kind of. I met Mr. Johnson, Jr., at last month's charity mixer. I was helping out the caterer. He was kind enough to take a picture with me once he found out I am one of his longtime fans," she said, smiling.

"But this is my first time meeting Mr. Johnson, Sr."

"Okay." Trevor smiled. "Wesley J is never too busy to show appreciation for his fans," he said like a proud uncle. Dad gave me a knowing look, but thankfully, he chose to stay silent.

After all the pleasantries, we sat down at an oval-shaped

conference-style table in Trevor's office. I had trouble keeping my eyes off of Serenity. She looked so good first thing in the morning. She had her thick beautiful hair pulled back away from her face, cascading down her back in soft pillowy curls. She wore a soft peach-colored dress that hit just above her knees, and it fit her to perfection. She wore nude-colored heels with those pretty toes painted with white nail polish. Her skin looked silky-smooth and glistened like she dripped liquid diamonds all over it. I could smell her warm vanilla fragrance from across the table.

"Son?" my dad's voice interrupted my silent evaluation of Serenity. "What do you think?"

All eyes were on me. I was so focused on trying not to focus on Serenity that I had no clue what they were talking about. "I'm sorry, Pop, what was the question?" I asked, much to his amusement.

"How about we let you three think things over for a few minutes while we step out? It's a lot of information to take in first thing in the morning," Sharon said, saving me from any further embarrassment. "Serenity and I will be back shortly."

We all stood as Serenity and Sharon rose from their chairs to exit the room. Once the door was closed, Trevor and Dad looked at me and laughed. I shook my head. "It's not funny, Pop. I didn't know she would be here! I didn't know she worked here!"

Trevor, looking confused, asked, "So she's not a fan you ran into?"

"She's the young woman my son has not stopped talking about since he ran into her last weekend. And from the looks of it, I think he's a bigger fan of hers!"

"She kept it business-like. But, Son, you need to work on your game face!"

The older gentlemen ragged on me a little more before Serenity and Sharon came back to the room. I assured my dad that I would pull myself together and get focused so that we could get through the meeting. He was more tickled by my boyish behavior than anything. Watching Serenity in her element was so intriguing. At some point, I forgot she was the most beautiful woman in the room, and I was fully engaged in her presentation. Not only could she get the attention of any man she wanted, but she was also a true expert in financial advising. She shined. Her confidence and intellect made her that much more appealing to me.

We finished up our appointment right before noon. Trevor called security to escort us back down to the lobby. We said it wasn't necessary, but he insisted. While waiting for security to arrive, I walked up behind Serenity, who was talking to Sharon, and tapped her on the back of her arm. She turned to me, then turned back to Sharon, and said, "I'll stop by your office to finish up tomorrow if that's okay?"

Sharon looked at me, then looked at Serenity, and gave us an approving smile before saying, "That's fine. I'll see you tomorrow, Renny. It was nice to meet you, Wesley."

"You, too," I replied.

"So, *Renny*," I said, copying Sharon's nickname for her. "Do you make a habit of surprising people, or is it just me?" I asked, with my eyes on hers.

She smiled. "I promise I didn't know the appointment was for you and your dad until this morning. When I found out, I didn't tell you because I wanted to see the look on your face when you got here! And you did not disappoint!" She laughed.

"Okay, you got me. You got me good," I conceded. "Your presentation was very impressive, by the way."

"Thank you," she said, nudging her shoulder into my arm. "Hey, can you introduce me to your dad? Like for real introduce me, not like all business-like? I want to thank him for the flowers."

"Yeah, no problem. Hey, Pop! Can you come over here for a minute?" I summoned, breaking up his conversation with Trevor.

Dad walked over with a swag that was just inherent at this point, bypassed me, and went right into hugging an awaiting Serenity. Pop could just tell when someone was having a fan moment over him. *What in the hell? Dad just doesn't know how to turn it off.*

While she was feigning over him, thanking him for the flowers, and saying how much her mom loved him, I just stood there and watched like a prop in the background. Dad loved this type of stuff; he ate it up. I didn't blame him, though. He earned it. Serenity wanted to take a picture with Dad. But she had left her phone in her office, so I just used mine.

I noticed the security guard standing in the doorway, so I tapped Dad and asked him if he was ready to leave. He shook Trevor's hand and proceeded to walk out the door. "I'm going to stay back for a few minutes, Pop. I'll call you later," I said, not taking my eyes off of the woman of the hour.

"Okay, Son. Serenity, nice to meet you, young lady," he said, walking away.

I noticed the security guard was still standing in the doorway after Dad had walked out of the office. He had his eyes locked in on Serenity, completely unbothered by the fact I was watching him stare. I shifted my eyes to Serenity and then back at him. I walked over to him with my hand extended and said, "Hey, man, I'm Wesley."

He gave me a quick stare before shaking my hand and said, "Julian. Nice to meet you. Big fan."

"Thanks," I said with little emotion.

He looked over to Serenity again before looking back at me. "Well, let me go get Mr. Johnson downstairs. Serenity, it's nice to see you," he said, looking at her like she was the last supper before joining Dad down the hall.

I turned to look at Serenity, expecting her to answer for his behavior. It was obvious something was going on between them. I wanted to ask, but Trevor was still in the office, and maybe it wasn't my business. "Would you mind walking me to my office?" she asked.

I nodded and said goodbye to Trevor. The walk to the elevator with Serenity was a quiet one. She hit the down arrow before looking up at me. "He's not my boyfriend," she offered.

The elevator doors opened, and we got in. She pressed the button for the 4th floor. We arrived quickly. Walking to her office, I asked, "He's not your boyfriend, huh? Does *he* know that? Cause ol' boy was looking at me like he wanted to jump on me!" I tried to joke, forcing a smile.

We entered her office and sat down. "We only went on one date," she said.

"Just one? And he's acting like that? Damn, girl! I gotta be careful with you!" I teased, trying to lighten the mood.

She laughed a little and said, "But I am not seeing him anymore, so there's no need to worry about him taking my attention."

That statement made me smile. "So, are you getting ready to have lunch?" I asked, changing the vibe in the room.

"Um, no. I'm actually leaving here in a few minutes. I have an appointment this afternoon."

"Is everything okay?"

"Yeah, it's just something I need to take care of."

"Okay, well, do you want to have lunch after? I have to meet up with D, but I can see you when I'm done."

"I would love to, but I'm just going to go home after my appointment. I need to make a few calls and handle some paperwork. Thank you, though." I caught her eyes on me. "You need to save all of your charm for Saturday, anyway!" she reminded me.

"Don't worry about that! All I need you to do is be ready at 5:30 p.m., and I'll take it from there." A smile spread across her pretty sun-kissed face at my directions for our date. "Can I at least walk you to your car if that's okay?"

"Sure, just give me a few minutes. Oh, and don't forget to send me those pics of your dad and me. My mom is going to love them!"

When she walked by me to leave her office, I gently grabbed her arm and pulled her into a hug. "I've been wanting to do that since I saw you this morning, and you look really good in this dress, too," I said. *Because, damn!*

She lifted her chin. "Thank you. You look good, too, in your blue suit. I like this look on you."

I released her from my embrace. "You ready?" Serenity and I walked through the lobby, chatting and laughing with one another like old friends. We were close to the security desk where that guy, Julian, was standing and acting like he wasn't watching us, but he was. She became quiet, seemingly not wanting to make him uncomfortable as we walked out of the door. He and I silently acknowledged one another when we walked past him. I held open the door for her, glanced back at him, and said, "See you, man," returning my hand to the small of her back and exiting the building.

Chapter Thirteen

Serenity. Wednesday morning before the meeting.

Maya and I stayed up late last night catching up on everything that's happened in less than a week. Both of us had gone from single and waiting to dating and busy. Maya said she and Darren talked and texted constantly. She learned he was divorced with a six-year-old son named Ryan, who he sees every other weekend and talks to at least twice a day while they're apart. Maya sounded like a whole new woman when she talked about Darren. I was happy for her; I just didn't want her to move too fast with him. She was the type who loved hard, and I wanted her to protect her heart. We also discussed my conversation with Julian and how he said if I were not dating him exclusively, he would rather wait until I could be all in with him. Maya was impressed with Julian's confidence and appreciated a man who knew what he wanted, but still assured me that I made the right decision by being upfront with him. She reminded me to take my time and figure out what I really wanted.

I arrived to work at my usual time and felt tense when I saw Julian on duty this morning. I had somehow missed seeing him yesterday, but now he was only a few feet away from me. I don't know what it could have been, but for some reason, I noticed how handsome he looked today. *Maybe it has something to do with that kiss he lit my entire body up with.*

I liked Julian. I didn't want things between us to be weird, so I decided I would act normal. We made eye contact, "Good morning, Serenity," he said, sounding bland.

"Good morning, Julian," I returned, matching his energy. We paused, then I said, "Well, have a good day."

"You, too," he said, giving me a lingering stare.

I logged in and checked my calendar for the day. The names of the clients for the high-profile meeting were updated a few minutes ago. "Wesley Johnson, Sr. and Wesley Johnson, Jr." I read aloud. The attendees were Sharon, Trevor, and me. I had met Trevor, a new advisor on the team, yesterday afternoon, and these were some of his clients he was bringing over from *Time is Now Financial.* I couldn't believe what I was reading. I immediately called Sharon. "Did you see who we're meeting with this morning?" I asked before saying hello.

"Yes, I did!" Sharon said, trying to keep her excitement at bay. "Wesley Johnson and his fine daddy! I wonder what he's like in person!"

We cackled for a few more minutes before discussing what we would cover during the meeting then ended the call. The meeting was scheduled for 9:30 a.m., and it was already nine o'clock. I was able to get my doctor's appointment scheduled for this afternoon, so I was leaving right after the meeting with Wesley and his dad. I was looking over documents when I heard his voice. "Hi, are you busy?" Julian asked.

"A little. Why, what's up?" I asked.

"I just wanted to make sure we're cool. After the other night, I don't want things to be odd between us," he said, gesturing his hands back and forth. "I felt like there was some tension between us this morning."

"We're good. Everything is cool. I appreciate you checking in on me, though. I don't want things to get strange, either. Thank you for checking in, Julian."

"Okay, then, I'll see you around," he said. I nodded, and he left.

Wednesday afternoon. After the meeting.

I waited in one of the always unnecessarily cold exam rooms at my doctor's office, wishing I had a sweater or a blanket or something. I was freezing. Dr. Emily entered, greeting me by name and asking, "So how have you been feeling?"

I was honest and replied that I had been feeling rundown and sleeping a lot lately. I explained that the more I slept, the more I felt like I had to sleep, and I didn't feel completely rested in the morning. We talked about my diet, stress levels, exercise routine, and family history.

"Any chance you're pregnant?" she asked.

"No, Dr. Emily. I've been celibate for the past eighteen months, so that's not an issue."

Dr. Emily said she wanted me to get some blood work drawn, and she would call me with my results in a few days. Until then, she suggested I take some time off of work, offering me a doctor's note if I wanted one. Though I didn't like missing work, and I usually didn't, I was not performing at my best since I had been so tired lately. I accepted the doctor's note for Thursday and Friday and would return to work on Monday.

Once I got home, I made my business calls and called my job to make all of the proper arrangements to be out of work for the next couple of days. Sharon assured me she would work as many of my clients into her schedule as she could. My boss told me to take care of myself and to let him know if I needed anything. I was grateful to work with such a reliable and trustworthy team. I twisted up my hair and changed my clothes before taking a midday nap. I was beginning to grow more concerned about my lack of energy. But for now, I just wanted to sleep.

I woke up late in the afternoon, having missed calls from my mom, Maya, Wesley, and an unknown number. The unknown caller had left me a message, so I checked that first: "Hello, my name is Marcus White, and I received your email about viewing the empty rental space downtown. When you get a chance, can you call me back so we can set up a good day and time to meet? Thanks again."

I will definitely ask Maya to handle that meeting. I texted Maya and asked her to come over later. I called my mom back but didn't get an answer. I'm sure she wanted to talk about the picture I sent of Wesley Johnson, Sr., and me that I sent her earlier today.

I called a happy-sounding Wesley back, only to hear a lot of noise in the background. It sounded like a party or something was going on. "Hey, Serenity! How are you?" he shouted into the phone.

"I'm good." I paused. "Are you at a party or something?" I asked.

The background noise had disappeared by the time he responded with, "No. I'm actually at the studio. My manager called and told me an artist wanted me to collaborate with them on their new song. So, D and I are here now, listening to the track."

"Really? Who's the artist?" I asked, fishing for details.

"I'm not at liberty to say right now. I'm not even sure if I'm going to do it yet. But I do like the track."

"Well, I'm sure you'll elevate the song if you decide to do it," I said, gassing him up.

"Thank you! Yeah, I think I'm going to lay down my vocals on it and see how it feels." I heard someone talking to him in the background, and then he said, "I gotta go. But I'll call you later on. Alright?"

"Okay," I answered.

Maya arrived at my house after 7:00 p.m., wine in hand, talking on the phone to Darren when she walked in. She gave me a one-armed hug, then easily navigated through my house to the kitchen. Before finishing up her call, she gave him a flirty laugh. When she hung up, I was sitting on the couch, eyeing her. "I see you and Darren ain't letting up!" I teased.

She looked embarrassed. "Renny, this man is too good to be true! He's smart, fine as hell, funny, fine as hell a good listener, fine as hell, a successful business owner, and he's a good father. Oh, and did I mention he's fine as hell!" Maya said, holding up her hand like she was giving praise. She poured two glasses of red wine and joined me on the couch. I laughed at Maya's assessment of Darren. "Anyway, what's going on with you?" she asked, settling down next to me.

"I don't know yet. I've been feeling really tired lately, and no matter how much I sleep, I just don't feel rested," I said with frustration.

"Did you look up your symptoms online?" Maya asked, taking a sip of wine.

"No! The internet will have you thinking you're going to die from a headache! I'll just wait for my labs to come back," I said, taking a sip of my own.

"You pregnant? Am I going to be an Auntie? You can tell me, girl!" Maya said.

I patted her leg. "You know I'm not doing that right now. It's been eighteen months. It's not as difficult as I thought it would be. I've been meditating, journaling, taking care of my mental and spiritual health. I thought I had things under control until Julian kissed me the other day. Sheesh! I thought I was going to tackle him!" I laughed.

"I thought y'all kissed on your date?" Maya asked.

"We did, but it was a friendly kiss compared to the performance he put on the other day," I said, fanning myself.

"Renny, I don't know how you do it. I tried that celibacy thing for two months, and that's as far as I could go! I was lying in bed one night, lonely as hell! I pulled out my phone and sent a text to my old faithful!"

"No!" I said. "Not Russell?"

She nodded. "Girl, he hasn't let me down yet! Uhm!" was all she was able to get out while obviously replaying a portion of her night with him in her mind.
"Well, I haven't told Wesley I'm celibate, and I didn't have a chance to tell Julian, either. I haven't dated anyone since Tony, so I've never had to tell anyone. I don't want to jump too far ahead if we're not moving in that direction, but I don't want to be misleading, either."

Maya put her almost empty glass of wine down and looked at me. "Renny, I've told you this a million times, and I'll tell you a million more if I have to. It's okay to let them work for your affection. Let them work for you. You're worth it. So, what if you tell Wesley you're celibate? What's he gonna do? Stop talking to you? If he does, that's his loss, not yours. Yes, he's good-looking, and he seems to have a lot going for him, but you have a lot going for you, too. There is a whole sea of attractive, successful men in this city who will treat you how you deserve to be treated now that you're ready to date again. Don't worry, be who you are and let the rest fall into place. You are the prize." Maya encouraged. We finished drinking our wine and having girl talk. Maya agreed to meet with the potential renter tomorrow evening with Darren accompanying her, so she wasn't alone.

We were reminiscing about some of our crazy antics in college when my phone rang. I smiled and held it up to face Maya showing her who it was. "Oh, shoot!" she said. "Put it on speakerphone!"

I laughed and answered. "Hi Wesley," I said, trying to sound extra cute.

"Serenity, I hope I'm not calling you at a bad time, am I?"

"No, I'm just sitting up here talking to Maya."

"Oh, tell her I said hi."

"I will. How did things go in the studio? Do you think you're going to do the song?"

"Things turned out really good, actually! I'm very pleased with the song, so you'll be able to hear it soon."

"I can't wait." Maya held her hand over her mouth to muffle her laughter. I think the wine had her feeling extra giddy.

"Do you mind if I call you back in a little bit? Maya and I were just finishing up," I said, with a smile that could be heard through my voice.

"Oh, y'all over there having girl talk, huh?" he asked, sounding amused.

"Yeah, and we're talking about you, so let us finish!"

He chuckled. "Well, I was just thinking about you and wanted to hear your voice," he said in a sweet tone. "I'll be waiting for your call later."

If I had looked up the word swoon in the dictionary, it would have been me at that moment, complete with a name tag and a Kool-Aid smile. "Okay, I'll talk to you then," I said before hanging up.

Maya and I burst out into laughter. "You think he knew you had him on speakerphone?" Maya asked, still laughing.

I shrugged. "I don't know."

"Renny, he sounds so sweet! I'm glad you have a chance to get to know the real him."

Chapter Fourteen

Wesley. Wednesday Afternoon.

After the meeting, I laid my vocals on the track in the studio for an artist named Young Problem. He was a young man with a huge social media following, a lot of money, and regular radio hits. His mom had been a fan of the group Xtascy back in the day, and he wanted to surprise her by having me on the track. I had done a few independent projects over the years, nothing mainstream, though. It wasn't every day I was asked to be on a record with a big-name artist like Young Problem and to be handpicked, no less.

I listened to the track a few times, and then I wrote the chorus and the bridge. I sang my part of the song until it was right and went in and added adlibs. I loved being in the studio. But since I'm somewhat of a perfectionist, the whole process was more time-consuming than it should have been. Young Problem lived out in LA, so we had to send the track back and forth a couple of times before he approved it. My manager would handle the business end of things and get back with me.

D and I rode back to his barbershop so he could pick up his car. "You figure out what you're going to do for your date this weekend?" he asked.

"Yeah, bro, I got it all planned out."

"So, what are you going to do?" he eagerly asked.

"That's under wraps! I know you talk to Amaya, and I don't want you to slip and tell her anything, man."

D's mouth dropped open. "Oh, for real, G? You think I would do you like that?"

"Nah, man, but I can't take any chances! But you'll know how it goes." D exited my car and made sure his shop was locked up properly before driving away.

It had been a long day, so I wasn't surprised I'd fallen asleep in my theater room, only to be awakened by Serenity's call. It was after eleven o'clock, and quite frankly, I was surprised she was still awake and calling me at that hour. "Hello?" I said in a low, sleepy voice.

"Wesley, hey, are you sleeping?" she asked.

"I dozed off for a minute, but I'm good. What are you doing up so late?"

She yawned and replied, "I've been binge-watching Netflix and got lost in the time. I told you I'd call you back, so I took a chance hoping you'd still be up. I hope it's not too late."

"No, it's not too late. I'm glad you called, but don't you have to work in the morning?"

"No, I'm taking some extra days off, and I'll still be working from home a little bit. So, tell me about the studio," she said as her voice perked up.

"It was like riding a bike. Sometimes I miss it—making music, touring, and performing, but there's no room out there anymore for the type of music I want to make. I love the old style of R&B. That good-sounding baby-making music! That's all my dad ever sang and played around the house when I was growing up. Don't get me wrong, there are plenty of artists out right now whose music I love, but it hardly ever gives me that feeling. You know?"

"Yeah, I know exactly what you mean. When I listen to R&B, I want to feel like the person singing is having an intimate conversation with me. Like it's something you would whisper in your woman's ear. When there's love in the lyrics, you can feel it. It makes you feel like it's just for you. Do you know what I mean?"

I had never heard the feeling of R&B music put quite that way, but I liked it. Then, I randomly thought about how good she looked in her office earlier today, and the feeling that got caught in my chest when our eyes connected. I smiled and replied, "Yes, Serenity. I completely understand where you're coming from."

"So, where does your songwriting inspiration come from?"

By this time, I had gotten up and gone to the kitchen to grab a bottle of water. "A lot of different places," I began. "The people around me, other artists, and personal experiences mostly."

"Well, you write a lot about love and relationships, so you must have a lot of experience in that area." I laughed out loud.

"Oh, so that question was a trap?" She laughed into the phone at my answer. "But really, I haven't had many serious relationships."

"What about love?" she asked. I paused, and I guess my silence invited her to say, "Oh, I'm sorry. I'm asking you too many personal questions."

"No, it's okay. That was a fair question. I have loved before," was the only answer I wanted to share. "What about you?" I asked.

She laughed and replied, "Same, I guess."

I couldn't help my curiosity from growing, but I didn't want to push. It was after midnight now. We were still up talking and getting to know one another. I can't remember the last time I had a conversation on the phone with a woman that lasted more than five minutes, but she was easy to talk to. I found myself floating in the sound of her voice, and her laugh made me smile. I already liked her. But the more we talked, the more she drew me into her warm spirit.

"Wesley, can I ask you a personal question?" she asked, sounding serious. I became nervous about what she may ask, but I said yes anyway.

Taking a deep breath, she asked, "How would you feel if I told you that I am …celibate?"

Her question completely caught me off guard. I took only a moment to answer, though. "I would say that I respect the choices you've made for yourself, and I would never try to put you in a compromising position."

Serenity sounded like she released a breath she'd been holding in, waiting for my answer. "Wesley, I know we're still getting to know one another, but I just wanted you to know what you're getting into with me."

"Serenity, I'm enjoying getting to know you. We can take things as slow as you need to. I wouldn't ever try to rush you to do anything you're not comfortable with. You're safe with me," I assured her.

Her confession made me wonder if that was why she and that guy Julian only went on one date. Had he tried to force her to do something with him? Did he make her uncomfortable? I tried not to let my thoughts get too far. "I'm glad you feel that way," she said, starting to finally sound sleepy.

"I'll let you get some rest," I said. "I'll call you tomorrow. Good night, Serenity."

Chapter Fifteen

Serenity. Saturday Night…the date.
I'll be the first one to admit I was still a ball of nerves for tonight's date with Wesley. We had talked on the phone every night this week leading up to our date, most times falling asleep on one another. I was getting more comfortable lowering the veil of his celebrity and talking to him like I would any other man I was getting to know. I was surprised to find out that, among other things, Wesley had a great sense of humor, and he was a phenomenal storyteller. Some of the stories he told about him and his group on tour had me in stitches.

We decided our date would consist of two parts. For the first part, Wesley would choose something outside of his comfort zone. And for the second part, I would choose. Maya stopped by before her catering event for the evening to help me pick out something casual and cute to wear. Wesley told me to wear sneakers or comfortable shoes for the date he picked out for us, making me think we would do a physical activity. I hoped that wasn't the case, though! For my outfit, I settled on a pair of light blue skinny jeans, a short-sleeved, cotton emerald green cropped blouse, and a cream-colored duster just in case it got chilly later on in the evening, and a simple pair of all-white sneakers. My hair had a nice braided out texture, so I wore it up in a loose top knot bun, and I swooped down baby hairs around my edges. Lip gloss, brows, lashes, and pearl earrings completed my minimal beauty look.

At 5:30 p.m. on the dot, the doorbell rang. Maya and I jumped as if we had forgotten we were waiting for Wesley to arrive. Maya went to open the door while I gathered my purse and essentials for the night. "Hi, Wesley. Nice to see you again," I heard Maya greeting him. "She's in there." I stood anxiously waiting for him to turn the corner and enter the living room.

The first thing I noticed when he entered the room was his smile. He had a set of perfectly straight white teeth. Then I saw the flowers, a gorgeous bouquet of purple tulips. I could tell that he had been to Darren's barbershop today by the way his beard was neatly sculpted, and his line-up was picture perfect. He wore a pair of black jeans and a casual designer button-up black shirt. The shirt had some type of faint abstract design on it that I could only see up close. The top two buttons of his shirt were undone, which gave me a glance of his chocolate, sun-soaked chest. He had on a pair of black and gray sneakers, not sure of the brand, and a simple yet expensive-looking gold watch. I noticed the few times I'd seen him that he always had on dark colors for some reason. And there was that cologne again, a scent that was like a magnet to my nose. He was serving all types of grown man energy, and I was here for it. I took him in with my eyes and silently caught my breath.

"Serenity, you look even more beautiful every time I see you," he said, kissing my cheek and wrapping his arms around me, tulips and all. He stepped back and said, "Oh, these flowers are for you. I chose purple because it's the color of royalty, my queen," he flirted.

I blushed hard. "Thank you, Wesley. I love the flowers, and you look very, *very* handsome, too," I said, struggling for words. *Wesley Johnson is really standing in my living room!*

Maya walked over to us. "Let me take those flowers for you," she said, giving me a *'damn, girl!'* look as she walked by.

His eyes scanned my home. "I like the way you've decorated your place. You have a unique sense of style, but that doesn't surprise me, though," he said, catching his eyes with mine.

"Thank you."

"Are you ready to see what I have planned for you tonight?" he asked, trying to remain cool, but I could tell he was excited. I looked over to Maya, who was standing off to the side like a proud mother, sending her daughter to prom.

"Yes, I'm ready. Maya, can you lock up for me, please?"

"I got you, girl. Have fun! Wesley, take care of my girl!" she said, in a you better do it or else type of tone.

"Don't worry, Amaya! I got her!" He said with all of the confidence in the room.

We walked outside to his awaiting black-on-black Mercedes Benz sedan. I wasn't too good at recognizing cars, but the freshly detailed emblem shining in the grill gave it away. He opened the door for me, walked around to the driver's side, and got in. We buckled up and drove off. He played a local radio station in the car as we engaged in casual conversation, nothing too deep. I'll admit, I was already enjoying the night, and I had no clue where he was taking me.

"Do you have a music playlist?" I asked.

"Oh, you don't like the radio?" He laughed.

"It's fine; I just want to hear the type of music that you like."

"How about we listen to your playlist on the way there, and we can listen to mine on the way back? Deal?" he asked, glancing over to me.

"Alright, that sounds like a plan."

He pushed the Bluetooth connect button from his steering wheel so that I could sync my phone. "Okay, don't judge my music!" I warned as I connected my phone.

"I won't, I promise," he said.

"This is one of my favorite playlists; it fits all occasions." The first song that played was "As" by Stevie Wonder, and Wesley's expression said he was already impressed.

"Okay!" he said, turning up the volume. It was as if we read each other's minds. We started to sing the first lines of the song together. My playlist went from the classics like Stevie Wonder and Aretha Franklin to current artists like HER, The Weekend, SZA, and Drake. I also had some ratchet songs in my playlist that Maya and I usually turned up to.

Soon, we were arriving in the crowded streets of downtown Charlotte on a Saturday night. Parking was always terrible, but we lucked up and pulled into a space someone was just leaving. Wesley looked over at me and smiled. He picked up my hand and kissed it, unbuckled his seatbelt, and came to retrieve me from the passenger side of his car.

Chapter Sixteen

Wesley.

I opened the passenger side door for her and helped her to her feet. I could get a better view of her whole outfit, from her hair down to her pretty feet that were, unfortunately, covered up. Looking at her made me involuntarily bite my bottom lip. The way the sun glided on her face made her look like royalty. I had no doubt her beauty was gifted down from kings and queens. I was instantly drawn to her glowing golden brown skin, full lips, and small frame. She was petite, but I could tell she ate all of her greens and cornbread growing up. I held her hand and walked to the building with a sign reading, *Forks Up.*

We walked into a large classroom-style room that had a total of six stations set up with ingredients and kitchen utilities at each station. Upfront, there was a large demonstration area set up for the instructor. Serenity turned to me with a bright smile. "We're taking a couples cooking class?"

I nodded, "Yeah, this is definitely outside of my comfort zone! I'm not good at cooking at all, but you've told me that you are. So, I figured you'd be able to help me along the way." A few people were already mingling around the space, so we made small talk with them before going over to our assigned stations to begin the lesson. No one there seemed to directly recognize me. However, a couple of people commented, "Don't I know you?" or "You look familiar."

After Serenity tied on her apron like an expert chef, she grabbed one for me and held out the neck loop, prompting me to lower my head so that she could slip it on. Then she took the initiative to go behind me and tie the apron in the back. "Here, give me your arms," she requested with a cute smile. She rolled up my sleeves just above my elbows and said, "Take off that watch and put it in your pocket or something. You don't want to get it messed up." I complied.

Then we went to wash our hands. I made sure we were upfront to get a close look at what the instructor was doing. I wanted to have all the advantages to make sure our meal came out well, and I wanted to impress her. I wouldn't tell Serenity, but I was a nervous wreck. I usually never got nervous.

"I want first to welcome all of our lovely couples to *Forks Up!* We're glad to have you with us tonight! My name is Alex, and I'll be your instructor for the evening. I believe cooking can be fun, and it's a great activity to do together," she said with enthusiasm. "How many of you here tonight are on your first date?"

Serenity and I gave one another a quick look, raised our hands, and looked around at the other attendees. All but one couple had their hands raised. "I see everyone is in good company tonight!" she continued, "And fellas, be sure to take good notes because women love a man who can cook!" she joked. Everyone in the class chuckled. "Tonight, each couple will be making roasted duck with orange hazelnut stuffing, braised cabbage, and mashed potatoes with caramelized onions. After we're done, you can sit down with your date or others in tonight's group and enjoy your meal. Dessert is already prepared for you. and we will be serving wine as the beverage. Any questions?" Once no questions were confirmed, we got straight into the lesson.

We had to prepare the duck first since it would take the longest to cook. I looked down at the raw bird and became a little overwhelmed. I'd never cooked a whole bird before, and I would need help. Serenity instinctively grabbed my hand and said, "We got this! We're going to have the best tasting meal here!" Her words calmed my nerves as we watched the demonstration on what to do. I followed along as best as I could. When I fell a little behind, Serenity coached me through the process instead of jumping in and doing it for me. I'm a hands-on person, so that method of teaching was perfect for me. She handled the majority of the chopping needed for the meal. I peeled and boiled the potatoes, chopped the cabbage, and kept the area clean while we cooked. We had a nice little system going, and I liked working with her. She made it easy and fun. Any excuse I could find to touch her hand or put my hands at her waist to move past her, I took full advantage of. Soon, we were cracking jokes and laughing with one another. The instructor must have been a part-time comedian on the side. Either that or she had too many sips of wine! She had the whole class laughing several times throughout her presentation. I was having such a good time with Serenity. Our connection was organic, and I felt like our meal would turn out well, too. All my nerves had disappeared. I knew I wouldn't have been able to prepare the meal without her.

"I'll let you be in charge of making the mashed potatoes," she said.

The bowl of freshly boiled potatoes looked up at me. "Are you sure?" I asked, hesitantly.

"Yes, Wesley! You've been doing really well with everything else. I'm sure your potatoes will be bomb!"

I gave her a lingering look after her last statement, taking her in. She was the exact opposite of any woman I had dated before. She was patient, encouraging, and kind. When I made a mistake, she just responded with, "That's okay. It doesn't have to be perfect," and suggested how we could work around it. She caught my eyes lingering on her. "What?" she asked in a sweet tone.

I wanted to kiss her right then, but I didn't know if that would be too much for her. So instead, I said, "Yeah, these potatoes are gonna be the best you've ever tasted!"

Chapter Seventeen

Serenity.

Wesley put forth a valiant effort in helping to prepare the meal. I could tell he was completely out of his element, but he still gave it his all. I saw his eyes fixated on me a few times while we worked together. I stole a few glances of him, too. Our attraction to one another was palpable.

Our meal was finally ready, and it was now the moment of truth. The instructor, Alex, turned on some jazz music and gave each couple a bottle of wine to enjoy with our meals. I sat at the table and poured the wine, a nice Pinot Noir, while Wesley prepared our plates.

"For you," he said, placing my plate in front of me and giving me a little nod for effect. I'll admit, everything looked delicious. I had worked up a big appetite smelling everyone's food cook during the class.

"This looks good, Wesley! I'm impressed by your plating skills!" For the first time tonight, I think I made him blush.

He held out his hand to mine. "I'll say the prayer," he offered.

I gladly accepted his hand and ended his prayer with an "Amen." The room was full of chatter, laughter, and the sound of silverware clanging. I picked up my knife and fork, ready to dive in, but he hesitated.

"What's wrong?" I asked.

"Nothing, I just don't know what to try first," he answered with a boyish smile.

"Let's try the duck first," I suggested. The stuffed duck was so tender and perfectly seasoned that we didn't even need words to express our approval. We engaged in a series of facial expressions, grunts, and pointing our forks down at the duck before taking another bite. Then we tasted the braised cabbage, which I made.

He smiled at me. "Mmm, this is really good!" he complimented before eating a couple of more mouthfuls.

Then there were the mashed potatoes with caramelized onions that Wesley made. He put some on his fork and extended it to me. "Are you ready to taste the best mashed potatoes you've ever had?" he asked, trying to joke but being serious at the same time.

I was hoping they would taste good because my expression would say it all if they didn't. I accepted his fork with a smile. When I tasted it, my smile slowly went away, and I stopped chewing. He sat, anticipating the verdict. "Wesley, what did you put in this?" I asked as kindly as I could.

I didn't want to come right out and say it, but these mashed potatoes were awful! His smile disintegrated. "You don't like them?" he asked.

"Uhm, they're okay," I said, forcing myself to swallow them. "It just needs a little more seasoning." His laughter took me by surprise. I was confused about what was so funny.

"Try the potatoes on your plate," he said, still chuckling. I gave him a confused look. "Trust me." I took a small bite and looked up at him.

He was holding a smirk as he watched me try them. "Better?" he asked. They were better. Much better. Absolutely delicious. "I wanted to see if you would tell me the truth if you didn't like my food or if you would spare my feelings. I didn't do anything crazy to them, though. I just didn't put any seasonings in it. I'm happy you told me the truth!"

I sighed in relief. "Wesley, that's not funny! You know you shouldn't play around with someone's food like that!" I laughed.

He got up, came around to my side of the table, and kneeled next to me. He held my hand and kissed it, "Will you forgive me?" he asked, giving me a look I couldn't refuse.

I acted as if I needed to think about it before saying, "Yes. I forgive you."

I saw his eyes being drawn to my lips, so I leaned closer to him. "May I kiss you, Serenity?" he asked, gently. I nodded. He closed the distance between us and gave me a soft, slow kiss. My hands inconspicuously trembled. He looked at me. "Thank you," he said, standing up and going back to his seat. That one simple kiss, our first kiss, warmed me.

We finished our meal, had the prepared dessert, an upside-down banana rum cake, and genuinely enjoyed each other's company. We mingled with the other couples in the class and thanked the instructor before leaving. When we got back to the car, we were all smiles. "That was so much fun! I would definitely do that again!" I said.

"I'm glad you liked it, and I would love to be able to take you again." Wesley had an easy gentleman charm I hadn't experienced before. He was calm, cool, and seemed like he went with the flow. He paid attention to me throughout the class and didn't seem bothered by me giving him instructions when he needed them.

I checked the time; it was after nine o'clock. "Are you ready for my part of the date? Although, I don't know if I will be able to top that!" I said, eager for us to go to our next destination.

"I'm ready!" he answered. I entered the address into the GPS, and we were only five miles away.

"There it is!" I said as we approached the lounge. This time, we had to park almost four blocks away because it was so busy downtown. That was okay, though. It gave Wesley another reason to hold my hand while we walked.

Chapter Eighteen

Wesley.

"The Carolina Lounge & Bar," I read the sign in front of the building aloud. I looked down at Serenity. "What do you have planned for us in there?" I asked, with all of my wheels turning.

"You'll see!" she replied. I trailed her into the lounge, where plenty of people were sitting under low lighting and semi-loud music. It was a nice place with a mostly over thirty crowd. "Can you go get us seats at the bar and order me a pomegranate martini, please? I'll be right there."

I made my way over to the bar and was able to find one vacant seat. I ordered her drink and a beer on tap for myself. She came over as soon as the drinks were ready. "Here, you can sit down," I offered. I looked around at my surroundings. "So, what's the plan?" I asked, taking a sip of beer.

She held up a small card with a number four written on it. "We are going to compete in a karaoke contest! You're a performer and I've never done anything like this. So, I figured this would be fun to try! Are you game?" she asked.

I was surprised by her choice, but I was game! Her excitement was contagious. I immediately started to think of songs we could perform to win. "I'm game," I said over the loud chatter and music, smiling at her.

"There's only one winner, and the prize is $500!" Now my competitive gene was starting to kick in.

Five contestants were competing, and the audience would decide the winner. "So, what song did you have in mind?"

"I am not sure, but something upbeat and fun! What do you think?"

We had about ten minutes before we had to give the bartender our song choice, so we had to think fast. We brainstormed several song choices before deciding it didn't have to be a duet. "I know what song we can do!" Serenity exclaimed. She whispered her selection in my ear, so the other competitors wouldn't try to mimic a similar song.

"Yes! That's perfect!" I went to the end of the bar and told the bartender our song choice. Plus, I gave him $50 to make sure he kept it to himself.

Serenity and I rushed over our strategy and pulled up YouTube on my phone to watch the music video of our song choice, pointing out which parts we wanted to emulate. Of course, it was all in fun, but we at least wanted to look like we were kind of prepared. The first contestant went up. She was a young woman who did a rendition of "I'm Coming Out" by Diana Ross, and she was actually good. The crowd was going crazy. I knew this wasn't going to be an easy win. I saw the unsure look on Serenity's face. I leaned to her ear and said, "Don't worry! She's good, but we're gonna win!" I winked and gave her a reassuring smile. Even if we didn't win, I was sure we would at least have a good time doing it.

The third contestants were finishing up, and Serenity finished up her second martini. *Liquid courage.* "Are you ready to do this?" I asked, with excitement building.

She nodded, and I led her to the stage area. Before the music started, I heard someone in the audience yell out, "Is that the guy from Xtascy?" And the crowd started applauding before our song started. To avoid any further interruption, I signaled the bartender to start the song. The unmistakable guitar riffs that opened Prince's song, "Kiss," began to play. The crowd went crazy on the intro part alone. To switch things up a little, Serenity and I decided that she would sing the song, and I would be her object of affection, which was the opposite of the video. She sang the first lines in her best imitation of Prince, playfully sliding her hand down the front of my chest. My already present smile grew even wider. I didn't mind being her stage prop; I think that moment was my most favorite time performing, ever! The crowd gave us a mixture of whistles and words of encouragement like, "Get 'em, girl!"

She circled me while singing the song, stopping at some points to dance up against me for emphasis. I performed right along with her, giving her and the audience what they wanted. I followed her body movements to make it seem like we had practiced our choreography. She gave me sensual looks, rubbed my beard, and pulled me down by the neck as if she were to kiss me during the chorus. She sang the line about wanting my 'extra time' before pushing me back. We heard the women in the audience yelling, "Kiss him! Kiss him!" But teasing me with the kiss made our performance that much better.

By the end of the song, I was seated on a stool. She finished the last parts of the song dancing in front of me, positioned between my legs, while I held on to her waist, still bouncing my head to the beat. She moved her body so well! I was pleasantly surprised by all of those sensual movements she had locked away! The last word of the song was kiss, so I took the opportunity to quickly spin her around, facing me, giving her a lip-locking kiss right on cue to end the song. Everyone was on their feet, and the cheering had grown so loud that we couldn't hear anything else. She wrapped her arms around my neck, and my arms were secured around her back. I stood, lifted her off of her feet, and gave her another kiss to seal the performance.

Chapter Nineteen

Serenity.

The crowd was still loudly cheering as we left the performance area. We were met with compliments and pats on the back while we made our way back over to the bar. "You were amazing!" Wesley said, hugging me. "You looked like you'd been performing that song for years!"

I laughed and said, "I have! In my bathroom in front of my mirror!"

He laughed, too. "Well, it paid off!"

We waited for the final act to go up, but the host announced that they decided they no longer wanted to compete. Wesley and I looked at one another and laughed because we knew our act was almost impossible to follow. "It's time to pick tonight's winners!" the host announced.

As he read the acts by song name, the crowd cheered more or less for their favorites. When he said the name of our song, the cheers indicated we had won by a landslide. I jumped up and hugged Wesley. "I told you we were going to win!" he exclaimed.

I went up to collect our prize money. When I returned, Wesley was circled by a group of fans, mostly women, wanting to take pictures with him and asking him questions like, "When are you going to make a new Xtasy album?" and "Do you come here all the time?" He made eye contact with me, acknowledging my presence. I nodded at him, giving him a look that said, do what you need to do, while I found a seat at a nearby table.

"You looked good up there," I heard a voice say close to my ear. "Thank you!" I replied, looking up to see the owner of the compliment. My heart dropped.

"You never did respond to my invitation, Ms. James. But I can see why," Sean said, motioning toward Wesley, who wasn't looking in our direction.

"What are you doing here? Are you following me?" I asked, standing to my feet.

"No. I canceled my party. Some of the guys and I came out to have a drink. Imagine my surprise when I saw *you* here with *him*." He smirked. "If you wanted someone with money, you should have called me. I got all you need and for you," he said, eyeing me up and down, "I wouldn't be cheap."

Thoroughly disgusted by his boldness, I began walking away from him. He gripped my arm, jerking me back toward him to stop me from leaving. "Don't be like that. I just want to talk to you," he said.

I looked at his hand holding on to my arm. His pulling caught me off guard. "Get your hand off of me, or I swear to God, I'll break it," I threatened.

He let go. "I didn't mean any disrespect." He laughed. When I turned back to locate Wesley, I didn't see him.

"You know, you have a real problem keeping your damn hands to yourself, man!" I heard an angry voice startle me from behind. Sean and I turned to see Wesley standing there, looking like he was ready to put in some work on Sean.

"Wesley! Hey, man! Look, I hope there are no hard feelings about that incident before. I hope we can still be cool," Sean said, sounding arrogant, extending his hand to Wesley. The look Wesley gave him sent a chill of fear up my spine, but I knew better than to interfere. Wesley stepped towards Sean, looked at his hand, and swatted it away like he was killing a fly.

Then, without warning, Wesley grabbed Sean by the collar, and Wesley's fist connected with Sean's jaw about three times before Sean's friends started to rush to his aide. A crowd started to form around the altercation. Sean was big, but Wesley was slightly bigger. It took two of the four people with Sean to pull Wesley away. Even then, Wesley could still connect a few more body shots, sending him crashing into a table before hitting the ground. Wesley landed a few kicks to Sean's abdomen while he was on the ground, too. I don't think Sean even had an opportunity to defend himself. Once security pushed their way through the crowd, the fight was over. Sean was on the ground among broken glass with his face bleeding and checking to see if he was missing any teeth. Wesley had broken free from the grip of Sean's friends, who seemingly didn't want to be involved in the first place. Anger and rage were still present on his face. Wesley didn't have any words for Sean; he just looked at the security guard and said, "We're leaving."

He walked over to me, examining my arm. "Did he hurt you?" he asked, still full of anger. I shook my head.

Wesley turned to the security guard, who was now helping Sean off the ground with one of his friends. "He assaulted her. He grabbed her by the arm and yanked her," Wesley said with force. I could hear his anger beginning to build again.

I grabbed his hand. His eyes softened a little bit when he looked over at me. "Wesley, let's just go," I whispered.

We headed toward the door. The music was still playing. Some patrons were not privy to what had just happened. When we got outside, he rubbed my arm where Sean had grabbed me. "Are you sure you're okay?" He asked, sounding much more subdued.

"Yes, are *you*?" I asked, inspecting his swollen and bruised hand. I gently rubbed his knuckles, "Come on," I said, intertwining his arm with mine and leading him in the direction of his car.

Chapter Twenty

Wesley.

I parked in Serenity's driveway after a silent drive from downtown. I wasn't as angry anymore. I hoped my actions against Sean wouldn't scare her away. I looked over at her, not knowing what to say. "Serenity, I'm sorry you had to see that. Sean and I had some unresolved issues that I tried to put behind me. But when I saw him grab you, all I could see was red."

She looked down at my bruised hand. "Why don't you come in? I can ice that down for you. I know it has to hurt," she said nicely, but with little negotiation. It was after midnight. Typically, when a woman asked me to come in this late, it was not to tend to an injury. However, tonight, I knew better.

I sat down on the couch while she went to the kitchen to get me an ice pack. She laid a small towel on my lap and another one over my swollen knuckles, then gently placed the ice pack on it. I flinched a little in pain. "Oh, come on now. Toughen up!"

Her comment caused me to laugh involuntarily, and it lightened my mood. "I'm going to go change. I'll be right back," she said once she ensured I was situated.

I pulled my phone from my pocket to check any messages I may have missed. I went on Instagram to see I was tagged in several dozen posts. Most of them were clips from our karaoke performance, which made me smile to relive our moments a few short hours ago. In the videos, my attraction to her was clear. I was looking at her like she was a cool drink in a desert. I clicked on another video, which showed my altercation with Sean. I couldn't see my face from the angle, but I was obviously the one in the video. I sighed, "What's done is done," I mumbled, knowing I wouldn't have changed a thing.

After grabbing a glass of water and a bottle of ibuprofen, Serenity came back into the living room. "Here, take this. It will help with the swelling," she said.

"Thank you," I said, taking the pills. She was naturally maternal, and I liked it. "We're online," I said, opening the video of our karaoke dance and showing it to her.

She chuckled. "Wow, look at us! You look like you were really enjoying yourself! Thank you for being such a good sport about it."

"You're welcome, and I did enjoy it! You surprised me, Ms. Serenity. I didn't know you were holding back all of that! You were turnt up!" I teased. We looked through a few more clips before she saw the one with the confrontation between Sean and me. Her mood shifted. She adjusted the ice pack on my hand. I sighed and said, "Let me explain that. I don't want you to think that I'm some violent guy who can't control his temper. That's not me. I caught Sean and Candice together that night at the charity event after you left. Before anything got out of control, my boy D came and pulled me from the situation. I was infuriated. Candice and I have been over since that night. And Sean—he was never my real friend to begin with. He's just one of those industry people who like to hang around those he thinks are important. He's a clown." I paused for a moment, then continued, "I'm not that guy. I don't want you to be afraid of me. I just got caught in that moment, and I hope you'll still want to see me after tonight."

Serenity's expression changed. "What's wrong?" I asked.

"I saw Sean and Candice together that night, too," she confessed.

I perked up. "What? How?"

She sighed and replied, "I went to the closet to lock up Maya and my purses. I had the key, but the door was already unlocked. I walked in, and they were—you know, doing whatever. I saw Sean's face because he looked at me, but I didn't know it was Candice with him until she walked up to us and stood beside you."

I shook my head, almost in disbelief. "So, Sean knew you saw him in the closet, and he still walked over to me like we were best friends asking me to meet you?" I bit my bottom lip, trying to control the anger I was doing my best to hold back. I turned my head to look at Serenity. "Is that why you said what you said to me that night? That I deserve better?"

"Yes, that and the fact I felt Candice's negative energy as soon as she entered my space. I'm big on paying attention to the energy people give off. I had just met you, and I thought I would have sounded crazy telling you what I saw." She rubbed my leg and continued, "I'm sorry that it happened. You didn't deserve it, Wesley."

I was silent for a moment. I needed to digest what Serenity just told me. This new information made me regret not moving Candice out of the way so I could get to him that night. Serenity removed the ice pack from my hand and gently rubbed my bruises.

"I'm sorry," she repeated, softly kissing my hand.

"Come here," I said, pulling her closer to me so I could wrap my arm around her. She laid against my chest, and I rubbed her temple with my thumb. "Don't be sorry; it's not your fault," I said in a low voice.

We sat still for several minutes with only the vibrations of our heartbeats. "Wesley," Serenity whispered, "I'm not afraid of you over what happened. I was surprised, but I'm not scared. Besides, you handling Sean like that tonight was sexy as hell!"

I let out a low laugh. "Oh, really?" I replied, offering my lips to hers for a series of three slow and passionate kisses.

"Yes, definitely."

Chapter Twenty-One

Wesley: Sunday, the day after the date.

I got home close to four o'clock this morning. Serenity and I fell asleep on her couch. When I awakened, she was comfortably nestled on top of me. I didn't want to wake her, but I knew I had to go home. At home, the sound of my doorbell woke me around 10:30 a.m. I found my phone and pulled up my front door camera to see who had the nerve to come to my house unannounced. "Unbelievable," I mumbled, snatching myself out of bed. "I'll be down in a minute," I said through my app. I went to the bathroom, threw some water on my face, and gargled with mouthwash before grabbing my robe and heading downstairs.

In anger, I opened the door to an impatient Candice standing there. "Candice, why am I not surprised you're here? What do you want?" I asked, completely unmoved from her undeniable beauty.

She held the screen of her phone up to my face. "Is she the reason you haven't called me?" She looked at her phone for verification. "Serenity James? Oh, what, you're dating fans now?" she said, in her familiar tone of arrogance.

"Candice, you and I are over. We have nothing to talk about. Who I decide to see is none of your business!" I said, trying to keep cool. "Look, I don't know why you're here, but you need to go."

She barged past me, entering into my foyer. "I came here to give you this," she said, snatching a watch out of her purse. "It's the watch your dad gave you, and you left it over my house. I thought you might want it back," she said in a nasty tone.

I took the watch. "Candice, thank you for bringing this to me. But this ain't cool." I opened the door even wider. "You need to go!"

"I also came here for this," she said, untying her long sweater wrap-looking garment to reveal she only wore red lingerie underneath. She knew how I felt about the color red. Where red normally meant stop, for me, it meant to go. The way her voluptuous body peaked through the barely-there garment, teased me. It tempted me. It was only then I realized she also had on red bottom heels, red lipstick, and red nail polish, too. It was too early in the morning for her to play games with me like this. My eyes said what my mouth wouldn't. It had been over a month since she and I split up, and I hadn't been with anyone else since.

I took a deep breath and silently prayed for strength. "Candice," I said, barely audible.

"Come on, *Johnson*, I know you miss me. I know that's why you got into that fight last night with Sean. It was over me. You still want me. You can say it, or I can beg you to say it. I know you like how I beg," she said in a sexy voice. Too damn sexy. She slid her fingers down my bare chest with one hand and grabbed around the nape of my neck with the other before pressing against me, positioning herself inches from my face. The thought of her with Sean entered my mind. I grabbed her hands and backed her away from me.

"Candice, stop! I don't want you! This thing between us is over! That's it! Now leave!" She advanced toward me again. "Candice, cover yourself up, walk out of the door, and go home before I lose my patience with you!"

I ordered, melting away any chance of taking things further.

She reached out for me again. I caught her hands and pushed them down. Candice huffed. One would have thought I threw a drink in her face from the expression she made. "You're going to turn down all of this?" she asked, dropping her sweater and giving me a 360 so that I could get the full picture. Her display had the opposite effect of what she desired. I got angrier. I picked up her sweater and shoved it in her hands.

"Candice, did you bump your head and forget that you were screwing another man in a public place while we were together? Has that conveniently slipped your mind? What happened? Did he stop spending money on you and now you're here looking for another handout? Now you're begging me for another chance? Listen to me! That will never happen, Candice! You only love yourself! You're selfish, and I don't trust you!"

She gave me a tear-filled stare. "Wesley, I'm sorry! I know I was wrong, but we can work this out!" she cried, lips trembling.

I didn't care about her tears. "How long were you screwing him, Candice? How long? Was he the only one? Who else were you with?" I yelled, asking her the questions that had plagued me over the past month.

"Wesley, please, don't do this to us!"

"Us? There's no us! There's you, and there's me, and I've moved on! I suggest you do the same! Now you need to go! Please, don't make me tell you again."

Realizing she was in a losing battle, Candice began putting her sweater back on, narrowing her eyes at me. "First of all, Wesley, you're not even relevant anymore, and I did you a favor by being with you! Your career has been over for a long time, and it will never again be what it once was! When's the last time you had a hit? You're still riding on the success of music that's over ten years old! Second, if it weren't for your father, people wouldn't even know who you are! You didn't have to work for success or money; it was handed to you! You call me selfish, but you're the one who's full of themselves!" she said, pointing her finger in my face. "When you realize everything that you're missing, you'll come back!"

She walked toward the door; I slammed it shut before she could exit. "Candice, you need to lower your voice," I said, lowering my tone. "You know I don't disrespect women, so listen to me very closely. The only person who ever tried to ride on the success of anything I created is standing here naked in my house begging me for another chance! You can say all you want. But remember, you needed *me*. I never needed you! And I don't have to sing any new hits. I write songs for artists who keep publishing checks coming every month! But you wouldn't know anything about that, would you? I have talent, and I'm a smart businessman. What do you have besides spreading yourself around the industry to the highest bidder? Maybe if you had spent your time trying to learn from me instead of trying to come up, you would have something that resembles a career! I'll always be relevant in this industry, and you'll always be fleeting. Remember that!"

I reopened the door for her to exit. She grew silent and didn't look at me when she walked past. "Oh, and one more thing." She stopped to look at me. "Don't ever talk about what my dad has done for me. You don't know anything about that." She stormed out, and I closed the door.

Her high heels clicked until I heard her engine start and her driving away. I didn't want to come at her like that, but she went too far. All that stuff she said didn't bother me, but I wasn't going to let her get away with saying it, though. I held the gold watch in my hand and blew out a hard breath. I hadn't even realized my watch was gone, but I'm glad she brought it back. My dad gifted me this watch when I got signed to my first record deal. I headed back upstairs to try and get myself a little more composed.

I tried to lie back in bed, but I couldn't rest. I picked up my phone to check any messages I may have missed last night. I didn't want to think about my confrontation with Candice or Sean anymore. I wanted to focus on the highlights of my night with Serenity. I wanted to think about her; the way her eyes softened whenever she looked at me, or the sound of her laugh, and that mesmerizing smile of hers. And her lips… her soft, full lips. I appreciated how I didn't have to spend a grip of money just to impress her, even though I would have. She appreciated my effort. When those women came up to me at the bar last night, she gave me my space and respected them; which meant she wasn't threatened by their presence. That showed me she was confident, and secure with herself.

I saw a few texts from D and my dad, which was pretty standard, but I'm sure they had heard about the fight last night and wanted to check in on me. I would call D later. But first, I called Pop and spoke to him for a long while about what happened. Though he didn't like that I ended up resorting to violence, he understood. I told him everything else about the night, and he said, "Son, Serenity could be good for you. I like her."

After talking to Dad over a cup of coffee, I checked my email. My manager had sent me the finished song I did with Young Problem. It was set to be released in three weeks. He needed me to fly out to LA to do some promo early next week. *These new cats work fast.*

It was no problem to go to LA for a few days. It would be nice to go to the West Coast for a change. I started looking at the videos and pictures again from last night. That was hands down the best first date I'd ever had. Dating without sex was something I'd never done. But when I remembered how I felt when I looked into her eyes, and kissed her lips, I knew Serenity was worth it. Since snippets from our date had been posted online, I thought about how her life would now be the public's interest. Being talked about was a part of my life, not hers, and I wanted to do my best to protect her.

"Hello?" Serenity answered from the other side of the phone.

Hearing her voice made me wish I was still there with her. "Good morning, Ms. James. How did you sleep?" I asked.

"I slept okay. I'm still a bit tired, but I have all day to rest. How's your hand?"

"It's okay; it's still a little sore and swollen, but it'll be alright." I paused. "I think your kisses helped make it feel better last night." *What was I saying? Did I really just say that corny line to her? This girl had me out here acting brand new!*

She laughed. "That's sweet. Well, if it's not getting better, I'll see what I can do for you," she said, playing along. "Wesley, I don't think I really had an opportunity to tell you how much I enjoyed our date last night. I really enjoyed myself. Even after what happened with Sean."

I smiled. "Oh, yeah? Well, when can I see you again?" I asked, not wanting to waste any time.

"Well, you know I work during the day, so I'm free most weeknights and weekends."

"Okay, that sounds good. I actually have to fly out to LA next week on business for the song I did with Young Problem, so I'll definitely plan something for this week. Is that cool?"

"Yes, that works for me. Oh, and before I forget, I want to donate the $500 prize we won last night to the Boys and Girls Club you volunteer at, if that's okay with you. I'm sure they can put it to good use."

My heart swelled at her thoughtfulness. She genuinely cared about others, and I loved that quality about her. "That's fine with me. I just need to make sure they still want me to volunteer after the video of the fight gets into their hands."

"Oh," she said. "Well, I know there's more to it. But at that moment, you were defending me, so that should count for something."

"I hope they see it that way too," I said, looking down at my injured hand.

Chapter Twenty-Two

Serenity.

Sunday evening.

Maya could not wait to come over and indulge in all of the details from last night's date with Wesley. She sat on the edge of the couch, ready to hang on to my every word. She knew what I had planned for my part of the date but was excited to know how our couples' cooking class went and exactly how he ended up in a fight at a bar.

"Maya, he's so much different than what I thought he would be. Even after talking to him on the phone last week, I still didn't know what to expect. He is so sweet, and he was a complete gentleman all night."

"I saw that karaoke song y'all did last night! Y'all looked real comfortable with each other! I'm sure he wasn't thinking about being a gentleman with you gyrating all over him!" Maya joked. We laughed.

"I know, but it was all in good fun! We had such a good time up there!" I said, watching a clip of the video on my phone.

"It was fun for you, but it was research for him! Trust me!" Maya concluded. "But, Renny, I am really happy for you. You went from not wanting to date anyone to having two equally attractive men taking you out on dates. I'm glad you're getting out there and enjoying yourself again," Maya said in a sweet voice.

"Me, too. I just need to take my time and really get to know him. I don't want to end up in a bad situation again." Making that statement brought up residual feelings from the ending of my last serious relationship with my ex, Tony.

Anthony "Tony" Harris was my first true love, and the only man to ever break my heart. He and I met the summer before I went into my senior year of college. Maya and I attended an afterparty for a free outdoor concert downtown. Tony and his friend, Dontaé, came over and introduced themselves to us. He was the finest man I had seen all night; tall, smooth caramel skin, athletic build, and colorful tattoos that peaked from under his tight-fitting shirt. He had jet black locs that framed his face and a smile that introduced him before he spoke a word. He was gorgeous. His confidence was on a million, and he looked like the type of man that wasn't used to women telling him no. He caught my eye, but I've always needed more than a handsome face to keep my attention.

He gave me one of the corniest pick-up lines I'd heard all night with, "I think you dropped this," referring to his phone number. He didn't have good game. Honestly, he didn't need it as good as he looked. I was certain women fell at his feet just from his presence.

I declined to take his number, countering with, "No thanks, I already got one." My rejection of Tony's weak game made him even more determined to pursue me for the rest of the night. He gave me all of his attention while ignoring every woman who desperately scavenged for his attention. Eventually, he wore me down through his charm and persistence that night. His friend, Dontaé, on the other hand, had no luck with Maya. As soon as Maya found out Dontaé was between jobs and living with his mother, he might as well have disappeared into thin air. Tony, however, was on his grind. He worked an office job during the day, and was building his own clothing brand, *The Imprint,* at night. His clothing line was centered around casual-wear sweatpants and athletic gear designed to highlight and enhance a man's endowment, along with his other attributes.

We played phone tag for almost five months before I saw him again during my Thanksgiving break from school. He invited me to meet him for lunch, and we ended up talking for hours. I knew the waitress was annoyed that we held up her table, but Tony made sure to give her a big tip for her inconvenience. Tony was sweet, and a perfect gentleman, but he didn't seem like the relationship type. My focus was on completing my bachelor's degree program before starting on my master's and me trying to date him would have been a distraction. Besides, Tony was never at a disadvantage when it came to getting women. His Instagram feed told that story for him.

Our one date turned into two, then three, then four. Before I knew it, I was counting down the hours until the weekend came so I could see him again. After dating for two months, he professed his love for me, and asked me to spend the night with him for the first time. I wanted to, but I hesitated. At twenty-two years old, I was still a virgin, and I had never felt like anyone was worthy enough to give myself to before Tony. My parents were very old-fashioned. They drilled the idea of no sex before marriage into my mind before having sex was even a thought to me. Sure, I had boyfriends before, but they all ended up being more like friends, never getting further than kissing and some occasional heavy fondling. However, Tony was different. He ignited a feeling of vulnerability in me that was foreign, but welcome. His energy pulled me into his aura, and I couldn't get enough of him.

We stayed up late nights talking about our goals and planning our future together. The night I decided to give my body to him, my heart changed. My first time was not at all what I expected it to be. He wasn't exactly romantic, but he was gentle and patient. The experience was uncomfortable and a little painful. After the tenth time, he had complete authority over my body, and my mind when I was with him. Our relationship quickly grew into something that I couldn't see myself being without. I fell in love with him, and he was my world.

Once I graduated from college, I began working full-time. Tony was traveling more because his clothing line was starting to gain some traction among a few A-List entertainers. I helped him plan his business finances and I connected him with a few people I knew could help him get his name out into the public. Shortly after I bought my first condo, I began getting messages from women about them being with Tony while he was out of town. I confronted him about it, but he denied that anything had gone on, and assured me that his interactions with them were all business related. After I showed him the proof one of his women so graciously messaged me, he admitted to his transgressions. That was the first time we broke up. He begged me to take him back, and in my moment of weakness, and the imprint bulging from his *Imprint* sweatpants, I gave in. He knew how to work my body over so well, that I'm sure it should have been illegal. I forgave him over and over again. No matter how many times he lied, or cheated, I let him right back into my heart and in between my legs. We went through this toxic cycle for five years.

I spent most of my twenties trying to be good enough for a man who didn't respect me, or the love I gave him. He said he loved me, but I now know that wasn't love. It was control and manipulation; and I was too green to recognize it. I was smart in every other aspect of my life, but I was so stupid for him. It wasn't until a pregnant woman showed up on my doorstep on a Saturday afternoon, claiming Tony was the father of her child, did I finally have enough. After the woman left, Tony admitted that he knew the woman, and he in fact could be her child's father. I broke down. With nowhere left to hide, years of pain and deception finally broke through. I felt the physical pain of my heart breaking. He tried to console me, but I slapped him across the face as hard as I could and told him to get out of my house. He quickly recovered and held me in a bear hug. He apologized to me repeatedly through my inconsolable tears to no avail. His apologies turned into kisses on my neck and his bear hug turned into a gentle massage between my legs with his fingers. It was the way he always got me to forgive him; through sex. He easily lifted me and carried me to my dining room, sitting me on the table. He spread my legs and pushed all 10 inches of his thick manhood inside of me until my cries turned into moans. I grabbed a handful of his locs, and I was stuck between wanting to snap his neck and wanting to pull him closer. "I hate you, Tony! I hate you!" I cried out in pleasure and in pain.

Only for him to respond, "I know you hate me! I know I ain't shit! I'm sorry, baby!" in a voice full of passion that would usually make me melt. That night, he hit spots inside me that he'd never reached before. He spent the rest of that night, the night I decided would be our last night together, apologizing to me in the way that only he could.

After Tony, I knew I would have to ease into any relationship I chose to be in from that point forward. Tony used sex as his power over me. Sex clouded my judgment and it always left me feeling worse after it made me feel good. He took advantage of my inexperience and kindness. I was left broken into pieces that became pulverized. I wasn't sure how I would get over Tony, but I did know that I would never allow any other man to have that much power over me again. Living through the break-up had me feeling the most depressed I had been in all of my life. Not even Maya was able to convince me to leave Tony alone for good over the years we were on again and off again, but she was always there for me no matter what. She helped me pick up the pieces. However, the grueling process of rebuilding myself had made me even stronger than I was before.

"I just can't help but wonder if this thing with Wesley is already too good to be true. The beginning is always the best. The best dates, the best laughs, the best kisses and hugs, everything. What if this is as good as it gets, Maya?"

Maya rubbed my arm to comfort me. "Renny, you're overthinking. It's only been one date. Let it breathe; let it grow and see where it takes you. I know you're afraid of being hurt because of what Tony did. But Wesley is not Tony. If you're truly ready to start dating again, you have to be willing to open your heart and let the past go. You're not the same person you were after Tony. You're stronger. I see you love yourself more than you ever have. Just be open to someone caring about you and doing everything in their power to make you happy." I sniffled. Maya continued, "I like Wesley, and I can tell that you do, too. So just go with your heart and give him a chance."

"I'm just so afraid, Maya," I said with tears in my eyes.

She reached over to hug me. "Don't be afraid, Renny. Maybe Wesley is the one; maybe he isn't. But at least allow yourself to be fully present with him."

"I know, you're right," I said, wiping away tears. Maya helped me put things into perspective. During my dark time, as I call it, I went to therapy, learned how to meditate, prayed relentlessly, and began journaling, among other things. I made up my mind I would never mentally go back to that dark place. Ever.

"Now!" Maya said, changing the topic and pulling out her phone. "I need all the juicy details! You had a date with Wesley Johnson from Xtsacy! He's your dream man! I want to know what he's really like! Let's talk about how he kisses, because I saw the video from last night! Also, we need to discuss how you held your composure looking at that fine man all night! And, how in the world did he turn into Mike Tyson in the middle of the bar?! Spill the tea!" We laughed.

After I filled in Maya on the details of my date with Wesley, we caught up on the latest with her and Darren's budding relationship, which seemed to still be going well. She also told me that we were able to secure the third tenant for our vacant rental unit. We agreed we would look into hiring a property management company to help us because things were becoming a little too much for us to handle on our own.

Maya left my house around nine o'clock. I was happy she came over and helped ease some of the doubts I had about continuing to see Wesley. Along with my mom, she always spoke encouragement and confidence over me. I often hoped I was as good to them as they were to me. I took out my journal and wrote a lengthy entry. Afterward, I decided to send Wesley a text message simply saying, "I miss you," because I did. I recalled what Maya said about being open and allowing myself to be in the moment with him, and it made sense. He made me feel good. He made me feel special like my happiness mattered to him. Though I didn't know if he would be the one for me, I knew I would not rob myself of the chance to find out.

Chapter Twenty-Three

Wesley.

Sunday afternoon

I called D to see what he and my godson, Ryan, were up to. If they weren't too busy, I would stop by before heading over to my dad's house. D invited me to come over, wanting to hear all of the details of my night with Serenity. When I got to D's condo, he and Ryan were playing video games. After greeting his little man and catching up on all of the latest playground gossip, D gave him a book to practice reading while he and I caught up in the kitchen. When I sat down, D looked at me with a devilish smile and said, "She already got you, dude! It's written all over your face, man!" I shook my head, but I could not disagree.

I told him everything that happened last night, from the cooking class to going to the karaoke bar. "Everything was going good until that dude showed up," I said, shaking my head. "When I saw him near her, I immediately stopped what I was doing. Then he grabbed and yanked her close to him! That was it for me. Maybe I could have walked away from him before that. But as soon as I saw his hands on her, I knew it was over."

"I wish I was there with you, man. That joker has always been jealous of you. That's why he keeps sniffing after the women you're with," D said, shaking his head.

"What did Serenity say about the whole thing?"

"That's the funny part. She was more concerned about my hand being hurt than the actual fight! She invited me in and gave me an ice pack for my hand," I said, feeling a little embarrassed and flexing my hand.

D's eyes stretched open. "That's what I'm talking about!" D laughed, causing me to laugh, too.

"I had to come clean with Serenity about Sean and Candice. I didn't want her to think that I go around acting that way like I don't have any self-control."

"You have self-control as far as not putting your hands on people; it's just your temper that would always get you in trouble," D said, shaking his head.

"Serenity told me she saw Candice and Sean messing around that night at the charity mixer, too. She said she walked in on them," I said, feeling like a fool all over again.

"Oh, okay. Now it makes sense that she said that stuff about you deserving better." D paused. "I like her! She seems like she's not into drama. I respect that, " he continued with a smile.

By now, D and I were having a drink, another one of his imported beer selections. "So, you mean to tell me you went out with this woman, gained access to her house past midnight, and nothing happened? Come on, man! I don't believe that! Nothing?!"

I couldn't hold back my laughter. "Nah, man. I told you; she's different!"

D laughed. "This girl got you out here cooking duck and singing in bars? My G! What's going on? I've never known you to do something so … normal! No shade! But you had a regular date with her. When you're really feeling someone, you roll out the red carpet to impress them! You're all with the expensive dinners, weekend getaways, and you're ready to serenade the clothes right off of them!" D said, sounding genuinely surprised.

"You're right. I can't deny that, but she doesn't seem to care about all of that stuff. She only cared that I put forth the effort to spend time with her, from what I can tell. Bro, I felt real corny booking that cooking class, but it was the best time I've had in a long time! I can't front. I don't feel like I have to put on with her. She's fine with me just being me. Plus, she was cool when a few female fans came over to me. She let me have my space to engage with them. Something like that would have sent Candice over a cliff!" I said, finding a little amusement at the thought.

Then I remembered something. "Hold up, D! What about you, though? You sat up in Amaya's house half the night and actually made it to her bedroom! You told me nothing happened with her, and I know you! You're quick to turn into *Mr. Let Me Help You with That,*" I teased. He took a sip of beer, realizing I caught him up in his own trap.

He sucked his teeth. "Okay! You got me! I see what you're saying. But still, Wes, I've known you for over twenty years. I've seen how women throw themselves at you. Hell, I've benefited from it! But you never really had to work hard to get a woman, at least not a quality woman like her. She seems like she's a real one from what you're telling me. She has her own, so she doesn't need you to buy her anything. She's gorgeous, so she has her choice of men. She stays in her own lane, so she doesn't need you to put her up on anything. You need to figure out what you can add to her life. You have to be willing to go deeper for this woman if you really want her."

Everything he said was right on target and had been things I'd thought about, too. *Do I have what it takes not only to earn her affection but also to keep it?* D always had the capacity to give me a perspective I needed.

"But I didn't even tell you the crazy part, man." I shook my head. "Candice showed up at my house this morning having a fit about me being out with another woman. Asking me, who's Serenity James? Women find out information quicker than the FBI! She showed up with nothing on but a little sweater to cover up her lingerie and wore red bottom heels. She saw the pictures online from last night, and it drove her crazy, man!"

D's mouth dropped open like this was the story of the century. He was all ears. "She what?" he asked.

"Yeah, man, dropped by unannounced, barged into my house, talking crazy, damn near naked. I had to kick her out! You know I don't do drama like that."

"So, wait, did she come by to bring drama, or did she step in and drop her coat, like boom?" he asked, still hyped up from the story.

I held up my wrist to show him my watch. "I left my watch at her house, and she was being a so-called good Samaritan by bringing it back, I guess."

"How did she look, though?" D couldn't stop himself from asking. I gave him a look that said this wasn't the time for that question.

He redirected. "Are you going to tell Serenity?"

"Serenity? Man, I'm not telling her that nonsense! I'm not trying to scare her off. Besides, nothing happened."

"I get that. But if Candice is irrational enough to show up to your house unannounced, she might show up to hers. I know you want to keep things peaceful because everything is new right now, but I don't want to see Candice mess things up for you. You might need to do some damage control. Think about it."

❋❋❋❋❋

Dad's house was about a forty-five-minute drive away from D's condo. His house was more like a compound. He had done well with his music career. Sometimes, he and his group still did special appearances for award shows and charity events. For the most part, he was enjoying retirement. "Hey, Pop!" I yelled when I entered the front door.

"Hey, Son! I'm in the office!" he yelled back. He had done a little redecorating since the last time I was there, and it looked official.

Dad looked comfortable in his recliner with a newspaper held up to his face. I sat down. "So, what's good, old man?" I asked, taking a large gulp of my bottled water.

"Just reading my Sunday paper, Son. So, I see you're looking happy today. Ms. James still has you smiling?" he asked, giving me a face only a father could. I talked to him about the date earlier today but seeing me brought the topic back up. I smiled like Cupid just shot an arrow through my heart. "That good, huh?" he asked, placing the newspaper down.

"Pop, this girl is special. I mean, really, really special. I just like how I feel being with her. Like, I can be myself and not have to worry about being Wesley the singer or the son of Wesley Johnson from the Midnight Stars. I can just be me, and that's good enough for her."

Dad moved forward in his chair and looked at me over his reading glasses. "Yeah, Son. I know that feeling. The right woman will have you feeling things and doing things you've never done for anyone else. That's how I knew I was going to marry your mother."

"Marry?" I almost choked on my water. "I just went out on one date with her, Pop. Let's slow down on the marriage talk!"

He laughed. "Okay, Son, you say what you want, but I saw how you were looking at her in Trevor's office the other day. You couldn't keep your eyes off of her. I know that look. That was the look of a man who was going to fall in love." I gave him a blank stare.

"Pop, everything that I know about her is amazing." I sighed, "But she did tell me something the other night that kind of surprised me." He waited for me to continue. "She's celibate. I told her that I had no problem respecting that, but I've never dated a woman with that type of situation going on," I said as respectfully as I could.

"Well, Son, is that a dealbreaker for you?"

I blew out a breath. "I don't know, Pop," I said, rubbing my hands over my head. "On the one hand, I respect her for setting that boundary. It tells me that she values herself and her body. On the other hand, it's hard for me to stop myself from wanting her in that way. You saw her; she's beautiful. I just never had any woman say that to me."

Dad laughed. "I knew I liked her! She's setting a standard for you, Son. A standard that you've never had to meet before. I'm not saying the women you've dated in the past didn't have any standards; they just never put them on you."

He had my full attention. "It's like this, Son—if you really like this young lady, and it seems like you do, you have to figure out ways to connect with her that aren't in the bedroom. There's so much more to loving a woman than just laying with her. Get to know her. Find out who she is and what makes her happy. Learn how to feed her mind, learn how to take care of her heart, show her you are worthy of her time and effort. Pray for her, pray with her, and protect her. You have to let her know that you can be the man she needs and the man you need to be for her."

Okay, so that was a mic drop. "Damn, Pop," was all I could say.

I visited with Dad for a couple of more hours into the evening. Everything he said about how I should approach my situation with Serenity hit home. Pop and D were right; I had been used to women throwing themselves at me since I was sixteen. I never had to truly work for any woman's attention. I know I'm a good-looking man, but when I added money, fame, and success to that, I basically could have my pick of the bunch when it came to women. Anything one woman wasn't willing to do, was replaced with another woman who would. That's just how it was for me. I calmed down a lot when I hit my late twenties. But now I'm thirty-five and can't say I've ever been in love. Dad and I talked about the new song I was featured on with Young Problem, and I told him I was going to LA soon for some promo stuff. Right before I was ready to leave Dad's house, I got a text from Serenity that simply said, "I miss you."

That text alone made me want to get in my car and drive over an hour to see her, just to say, "I miss you, too."

Dad saw the look on my face when I opened the message, "Slow down on that marriage talk, right, Son?"

Chapter Twenty-Four

Wesley: The following week, Tuesday afternoon.
Day 1 in LA

I touched down at LAX at 1:45 p.m., which made it 4:45 p.m. back home. Serenity and I went on a lunch date last week and talked on the phone almost every free moment we had. I stopped by her house last night to see her before I left because I knew I wouldn't be back until Friday afternoon. I can't lie; it was hard to leave her, even for just a few days. Before my trip, D came to my house, gave me a fresh haircut, and groomed my beard. Back in the day, flying into different time zones is something I never got used to when I toured. My body got all out of whack, and this time was no different. However, I didn't have time to dwell on how I adjusted to the time change; I had to get to work. My first stop was a photoshoot with Young Problem at three o'clock. Thankfully, I had car service because LA traffic is not something I wanted to drive in during my short stay.

When I arrived at the location, Young Problem's team had everything for the shoot, making me happy because I was ready to work. It seemed like everyone was there waiting on me. "O.G.!" I heard a young man's voice behind me say when I came out on set in my first fit. "I appreciate you coming out to do this with me, G! That track came out fire, bro! It's gonna be another number one!" Young Problem said, holding up the iced-out number one medallion on his chain to match his diamond grill.

"No problem, man, thanks for the love!" I said, doing the classic gentleman's handshake. Although Young Problem was young, all of twenty-one-years old, he was very professional when it came down to work. I liked his work ethic. Doing promo work could be draining. But he kept the energy up, and everyone was in a good mood.

Our photoshoot consisted of three different sets, meaning three different wardrobe changes. We also took several behind-the-scenes video clips to post on social media. Even though I was just featured on the song, everyone treated me like I was a main artist. I took pictures and gave recorded shoutouts to anyone I had time to do it for. At the end of the shoot, someone blasted one of Xtascy's biggest songs, "Dance Tonight," and tried to challenge me to the choreography! Light work! I had to let the youngins know that I hadn't lost a step over the years! It was all in good fun, and I'm sure someone recorded it. I felt the love from everyone there, but I was tired by the time I got back to my car. The next two days would be the video shoot and interviews, and then I would be on my flight home on Friday morning.

I had never been so happy to see a hotel bed than I was today. I was tired, hungry, and missing Serenity. I scrolled through a few pictures she and I had taken on our dates. I showered, then ordered room service; a simple burger and fries would do. I had a 7:00 a.m. call time tomorrow morning, so I had to go to sleep soon. However, I wasn't going to be able to close my eyes without hearing the sweet voice of Serenity on my phone. I decided to video chat with her instead of just calling, curious to see if she'd pick up. I laid back in the bed with one arm behind my head and the other holding the phone.

She answered on the fourth ring, looking as beautiful as always. My expression transformed into one of contentment as soon as I saw her face. Her skin was glowing, and her hair was wildly flowing. "Hey, you," she said sweetly, "how'd it go today?"

"It went well. I spent my day around a bunch of twenty-year-old's calling me O.G. all day, though! Made me feel like an old man!" We both laughed. "I had fun, though. It's just been a long day."

"Well, I'm glad you made it there safely, and I can tell you're sleepy."

I found myself just staring at her, wishing more than anything I could reach out and touch her. "What?" she asked.

"You look so pretty right now," I said without warning. She blushed. "I know I just saw you yesterday, but I miss you already. I wish I were there with you instead of across the country in this hotel room."

Before I left Serenity's house last night, I kissed and hugged her as much as she allowed me to. I typically wasn't an openly affectionate guy, but there was a pull she had on me that I couldn't explain. The affection we shared didn't get too heated or turn sexual, but the feeling it gave me introduced me to a type of intimacy I was eager to explore with her.

"I miss you too, Wesley." My heart skipped at her reciprocation. Yeah, she had me feeling things I had only heard about people feeling when they were really into someone. Now I was starting to understand those feelings more and more. We looked at one another for a long minute. She briefly told me about her day at work before I drifted to sleep.

Wednesday: Day 2 in LA: The video shoot
My 7:00 a.m. call time hit me like a ton of bricks. I had to get better at getting up in the morning. I texted Serenity as soon as I got up: *Good morning, sweetheart. Two more days until I see you. Have a good day.*

My car waited downstairs to take me to the video set. I showered, threw on gray sweatpants, a matching grey hoodie, sunglasses, and my backpack carrying all of my essentials. I grabbed a cup of black coffee from the hotel lobby then jumped into the backseat of my car. I had my hoodie up, leaned back to sip my coffee, and tried to catch a little more rest before we arrived. In this age of social media, many artists opted to drop singles without videos. But K'Vionne, aka Young Problem, never missed an opportunity to put his face in front of the camera.

This morning I would be shooting my solo spots, close-ups, long shots, wide angles, things like that. The wardrobe and jewelry the stylist pulled for me were top-notch. I had my choice of name brand everything. There were so many diamonds here. I'm sure there wasn't any left from where they came from. I had trouble deciding what to wear. I didn't want to look like I was trying to look younger than I was. I'm a grown man. I didn't have a desire to recapture my youth by putting on something that would make me look like I was trying too hard. I wanted to embrace my grown man swag. Thankfully, the stylist had me looking right.

The song's name was "Main Chick," so the video's premise was a man who decided he wanted to drop all of his side women to be with one woman, the *main chick*. My part in the video was pretty basic. I was in the car driving or at home lounging. I was pleased with how everything was looking when I saw the playback of the footage. It had been a little while since I'd seen myself on camera, and I looked good. I was glad I stayed loyal to my home gym workouts!

The afternoon shoot was reserved for my shots with Young Problem. I took a quick nap in my dressing room and had lunch while the crew set up. Around four o'clock, they were ready for me. This should be easy enough. There were two more sets and no more wardrobe changes. After this, I should be wrapped. We ran through the first set pretty quickly. It was a bar scene where Young Problem was caught up with his side chicks. We ran through the whole song three or four times before doing some cutaway and filler shots. We were feeding off of one another's energy. We had an organic vibe going.

The next setup was more, how can I say, visually appealing. The set was filled with young, beautiful, curvaceous women dressed in, well, hardly dressed at all. There were male extras, too, but they were clearly outnumbered. It was a house party scene. It wasn't X-rated or anything; I just hadn't been on a set like this in a while. "Yeah, O.G.!" K'Vionne yelled, coming up to me putting his arm around my neck. "Let's get this work!" he said, motioning over to the young women oiling up their bodies to make sure they looked good on camera. I knew this was just work, and it came with the job. But being all over these women would not be a good look. I wanted to be mindful that Serenity would see this video. It didn't matter if it was only for show. Indeed, the women were a vision that most men would step over their mommas to get to, but the only woman I could think about was Serenity.

The director, a young, skinny, Asian man with orange-framed glasses, came over to me to run down what he needed me to do before we started shooting. He said he made a last-minute casting for me to have a leading lady in the video, my *Main Chick*. That was fine with me. My energy was still good. I was ready to get it done. That was until he pointed over to the woman who would be my leading lady. I looked at the director as if his mind had jumped out of his head and went for an unsupervised walk. "Her?" I asked, wiping the prideful look from his face.

"Yeah, we were lucky to get her at the last minute. She's going to be dropping her new single with Young

Problem soon, so he wanted her in the video," he said, flashing a goofy smile.

The "her" was Candice. *What in the hell is she even doing here? Did she know I was doing this video and planned this?* I hadn't shown anything but respect for her since the breakup, but that little stunt she pulled at my house the other day went too far. My mood soured. The director looked at me confused, sensing my conflict. I'm not into public embarrassment, especially of women, but obviously, Candice wasn't getting the message. I'm a professional, but this was a reach, even for me. "Let me go talk to her for a minute," I said, walking away and not waiting for a response.

I walked up to her. She didn't turn her head to acknowledge my presence. "Candice," I said, shooting her daggers. "What are you doing?"

She turned her eyes briefly to look at me. "I'm working," she said with way too much attitude while applying lip gloss in the mirror. "Look, I don't want to do this with you either. But it's a job, and I'm going to do what I'm getting paid to do. I can be a professional. Can you?" she asked, looking at me like she wanted me to lose my temper.

"I know you, Candice, and I know you didn't just happen to end up here on the same shoot as me."

"Boy, I ain't thinking about you! You can go ahead and have your little plain Jane girlfriend and live happily ever after. I'm too fine to be stuck over you! I've already moved on from that little argument we had. I'm straight," she bucked back.

I clenched my jaw in an effort not to raise my voice. "You need to watch your mouth when it comes to her. You don't have anything to say about her. And I know you did this on purpose to get under my skin, but I can be professional and do my job. That's it, Candice. My patience is done with you. Don't make me embarrass you in front of all these people," I said, walking back to set, not giving her an opportunity to respond.

From afar, I'm sure our conversation looked calm and casual. Like I said, I'm not into public embarrassment. It was time to shoot, and Young Problem's energy was still floating on ten. He was doing his thing, and I could tell he loved the camera. The playback of the music filled the set while the extras were doing as they were directed. He reminded me of myself at that age, young, rich, talented, full of energy, and always around all types of gorgeous women. We were on the last couple of shots of the day for the house party scene. While I was singing the chorus and bridge, Candice danced on me while I stood against the wall. A classic R&B shot. It was sexy but not over the top. I could manage it. I did little flirtatious things like touch her arms and play with her hair while she danced in front of me.

Initially, she remained professional. Then on the last shot, she decided to face me and stroke my chin with a little grin on her face while looking back at the camera. Not wanting to mess up the shot or prolong the process, I moved her hand like it was a part of the choreography while lip-syncing. She must have taken that rejection as a challenge because she turned around and started to grind on me like she was trying to get pregnant. I was against a wall, so there was nowhere for me to move. I kept my hands off of her and just went on performing. I knew we were nearing the end of the take. Thankfully, I had a pair of dark designer sunglasses on, so my expression wouldn't be obvious to those on the other side of the camera. Right before the song came to an end, she turned around to face me again and was a mere centimeter away from my face.

However, this time, she grabbed my chin and turned my head toward her and licked my lips from the bottom to the top. It happened so fast that I was caught off guard. She smirked at me and scurried away. "Cut!" the director yelled. "Candice! That was hot, baby!" he yelled after her.

The crew applauded and whistled. At first, I was frozen and thinking, *What the hell just happened?* Once I came to my senses, I stormed off the set on a mission to find Candice. I don't know where she disappeared to so fast, but it was probably a good thing I didn't see her. As I breezed by the director, he tapped me on the shoulder. I wiped my mouth and turned to him. "She was being completely unprofessional, and I don't work like that!" I yelled, surely sounding like an adolescent girl throwing a tantrum. My father had taught me to always remain professional and keep a cool head in settings like these, no matter how mad I became. I didn't like how I continued to let Candice get under my skin. I couldn't understand why she felt so comfortable constantly testing me. Through all the chatter going on and the music still playing, I'm sure not too many people noticed how disgruntled I was anyway.

I went to my dressing room to change back into my sweats and call my car service. As far as I was concerned, this whole day was over. A few minutes later, K'Vionne came into my dressing room looking confused. "O.G., what's good, man? You out?" he asked, looking worried. "I wanted you to meet my mom real quick before you left. She's a big fan of yours, big homie."

Although the only thing I wanted to do was get out of that building, I could never treat a fan like they weren't important. Besides, it was Candice I had a problem with, not him and not his mother. I pulled myself back into a cooler headspace within seconds. "Alright youngin, give me a few minutes, and I'll be out there to meet her." After he left, I pinched the bridge of my nose to get myself together.

The video director stopped in to make sure everything was good and assured me they had all the shots of me they needed to complete the video. I told him I needed those last shots of Candice and me cut from the video. He assured me it would be taken care of. Usually, I would have had my manager put it in writing, but I took his word for it. I don't even think K'Vionne realized how abruptly I left the set because he didn't say anything to me about it. I'm sure his focus was on his surroundings.

K'Vionne's mother was an attractive woman with warm brown skin, big kinky hair, and a medium-thick build. She had on a lot of makeup, and I felt it masked her natural beauty way more than it enhanced it, though. But that's just my opinion. She was definitely the type of woman I would have gone for a few years ago. She had K'Vionne when she was sixteen years old, so she and I were around the same age. She was talking to her son when I walked up and said, "Keisha?"

She turned around with the biggest grin I'd seen all day from anyone. She squeezed me a little longer than just a friendly hug. "Alright, Ma. Alright, let the man breathe!" K'Vionne said, looking embarrassed.

"You're even more handsome in person!" she said.

"Thank you. I appreciate your love and support." We chatted for a few more minutes before taking a few pics and videos for the 'gram. "It was nice to meet you, Keisha," I said and turned. "Young man, I'll get up with you." I gave Keisha a parting hug and K'Vionne the gentleman's handshake, then headed out to meet my car service.

On the way to my car, I was stopped by the stylist, who had dressed me for the last two days. "These are for you," she said, handing me a heavy garment bag. "Courtesy of K'Vionne and his mother. It's the clothes from your shoot yesterday and a few extras."

"Thank you. I'll be sure to give them a call tomorrow to thank them personally." The clothes were top quality, designer pieces. I appreciated the gesture.

Thursday Morning: Final Day in LA. Home Tomorrow.
I was scheduled to call in to a few radio stations to talk about the new song being released with Young Problem. I could have done these interviews from the East Coast. But I was already here, and my manager wanted me to stay in town for any additional opportunities that might come up. For the most part, the radio hosts were gracious and kind, giving me props on my career and talking about my dad's legacy.

The last interview of the morning turned into a gossip column, though. "So, Wesley," the popular radio personality, Terry T., of *Terry's Morning Tea,* said. "I heard you shot the video for *Main Chick* with Young Problem yesterday. How did that go?"

"It went well. It was cool to meet K'Vionne. He's a really talented artist. I think his fans are really going to like the new song. I'm glad he reached out to me," I said, using all of the media training I kept on reserve.

"Well, we got some first look photos from the video, and you have a familiar leading lady there with you," she said, no doubt trying to be messy as hell.

"Yeah," I said without pausing. "Candice came in to be a part of the video. She and Young Problem have some new music coming out, so y'all be on the lookout for that,"

I said, avoiding where she was trying to take the conversation.

"Okay, Wesley, I see you're trying to keep it about the music! But a source tells me that you and she had some pretty hot on-screen chemistry. Is that true?"

I laughed. "Naw, it was all business, nothing personal," was the only answer I offered.

"I don't know, Wesley, you too were looking really comfortable from what I saw! Is there a reconciliation in the works for you two?" she asked, pushing it.

"No reconciliation is in the works for us, but I wish her all the best with her career and her music," I said in the sincerest tone I could muster. I've played this game many times before. I knew the host was just pushing for ratings and trying to get people talking about a story that wasn't there.

"Okay, Wesley, you're always the gentleman!" she said, backing down. "One more question before you go," she began, "the new song is called "Main Chick," and all the ladies want to know, do you have a main chick, Wesley?"

I chuckled at her persistence. "Right now, all I can say is that I am very happy. I'm very blessed."

"Okay, ladies, you heard it here first! He is happy and blessed, so please don't slide into his DM's! The new song and video with Young Problem featuring Wesley "The Gentleman" Johnson will be dropping this Tuesday y'all! Make sure you check it out! Wesley, thank you for joining us this morning, love!"

"You're welcome, be blessed."

Friday Morning: To the Airport

I stayed up as late as I could talking to Serenity last night, and I planned to go straight to her house once I got back in town. I decided not to tell her about my encounter with Candice just yet. I thought it would be better to tell her in person. Serenity and I were still in the getting to know one another phase, but I already knew I wanted to be with her exclusively. I had to make sure the timing was right. With Candice popping up every five minutes, I needed to make sure that was handled, too.

I walked down through the hotel lobby with my hood up and my shades on. I was getting ready to get in the car when a woman called my name from across the parking lot! "Wesley!"

I looked over to see Candice standing by a black Expedition like she was the queen of the world or something. This woman was completely out of control. How did she even know what hotel I was staying at? I figured this would be the perfect time to end this drama once and for all. I threw my bags in the car and asked my driver to wait for a few minutes. I walked over to Candice like a man chasing down his last dollar. "What the hell are you doing here? And what in the world were you thinking yesterday, Candice? You gave me a whole speech about being professional and not wanting me anymore, and then you do that?" I yelled because I just didn't care anymore. I was tired of her drama. She took the last piece of patience I had with her yesterday. With anger in my eyes, I stared at her, waiting for her response. She just looked at me through teary eyes. I couldn't believe she had the audacity to play the victim card.

I was raised to talk to and treat women with respect and love, so I had never cursed at a woman in my life. However, when I saw those crocodile tears vacationing in the wells of her eyes, I lifted my head to the sky and prayed for strength. *Lord, please, help me!* I begged when I should have been asking for forgiveness because of the things I really wanted to say to her. I calmed myself with a deep breath. "Candice, stay away from me. Period." I said, with no sympathy or acknowledgment of her phantom tears. "If you come near me again, I'm getting a restraining order." I shook my head in disgust, turned my back on her, and walked away.

"Wesley, I still love you!" She yelled, not stopping me in my stride. I opened the door to get in the car. "I'm pregnant!" I felt like I was frozen in time.

I walked back over to her. "You're what?" I asked, knowing good and damn well I heard her the first time.

Her tears began to fall. "I'm ten weeks pregnant, Wesley."

I looked down at her stomach and was speechless for a moment. "And you're telling me it's mine?" I asked in a voice that didn't seem like it was coming from my body. She gave me a regretful look. "Candice, you need to be honest with me. Do you think I'm the father?"

She started crying even harder. "I don't know, Wesley! I'm not sure!" She fell into my chest, sobbing uncontrollably.

Instantly, I got a headache. I rubbed her back. "Calm down. When are you coming back to the East Coast?" I asked.

She sniffled. "On Monday," she said through a stream of tears.

"Okay. Call me when you get back into town. We need to talk, okay?"

She nodded as I rubbed her back a few more minutes, doing my best to calm her before getting into my awaiting car. Suddenly, seeing Serenity didn't seem so exciting anymore.

Chapter Twenty-Five

Serenity.

A few days ago, I found out that I'm anemic, and that's why I had been feeling so lethargic. I'd made the proper adjustments in my diet, and now I was taking a supplement. I was feeling much better, but not at 100 percent, though. Wesley was set to arrive back from LA this afternoon and said he would come straight to my house from the airport. I was excited to see him, even though it had only been a few days since he'd left. Any free moment I had, I found myself thinking about different things about him that made me smile; whether it was his laugh, his warm hugs and gentle kisses, or the features compromising his beautifully sculpted face— all of it made me feel giddy inside.

Around one o'clock, Maya called me at work. It was strange because it was the middle of the day. "Hello?"

"Renny, are you okay?" she asked in a tone that made me feel nervous.

"Yeah, what's up? What's going on?"

"I guess you haven't seen the pictures yet?"

"Pictures? What pictures?"

"Of Wesley and that Candice girl! They were together in LA. You didn't see it? It's all online. I'm sending it to you now," Maya said.

I opened the pictures, and my heart sank. It definitely was Wesley, and that definitely was Candice with him. I assumed it was from the video shoot. But, "Is she licking him?" I asked out loud.

"Maya, I'll call you back," I said, catching a frog in my throat.

"Okay, girl, I'll be here," she said in an empathetic voice. I saw the pictures were on a gossip blog page with the caption that read, "It looks like these two are finally working things out!"

When I swiped left, there were five other pictures of Wesley and Candice that were obviously old. I went to Candice's page and saw she had posted the pictures, too, with heart emojis as the caption. I had talked to Wesley just last night; he didn't say anything about seeing her. Why wouldn't he tell me? I got a sick feeling in the pit of my stomach and felt like I was going to lose my lunch. I wanted to trust Wesley. But I hadn't known him long, and I didn't know what was going on. Had he gone there to meet up with her? Are they back together? I had too many questions with no answers.

Chapter Twenty-Six

Wesley.

I realized I could not wait until Monday to find out if Candice was pregnant or not. I checked back into my hotel room and told Candice to wait for me there. I then went over to the pharmacy and bought five different pregnancy tests and the biggest bottle of water I could find. When I went back to the room, it was obvious she had a different idea of what I intended to do with her. I dumped the pregnancy tests on the bed and looked at her. "Are you kidding?" she asked, almost sounding offended.

"Nope. Drink this and pee on these," I said without negotiation.

Irritated, she grabbed the tests and the bottle of water and went into the bathroom. While I waited, I pushed back my flight home. Now I would be leaving LA this evening, which would get me home close to midnight. I sent Serenity a quick text letting her know my change in plans. I sat in the chair, contemplating just how much my life would change if Candice were pregnant and the baby was mine. However, she had been unfaithful during our relationship. Although the time frame fit, I was not willing to take her word for it. She was not someone I trusted anymore. I felt like she would be willing to do almost anything to keep me as a part of her life or at least try to ruin mine.

My anxiety started to build. I knocked on the door. "Are you okay in there?" I asked.

"I'm almost done!" Candice responded.

Now, I was starting to pace. Ten minutes later, the bathroom door crept open, grabbing my full attention.

Candice stepped out with the tests in her hand. "Well?" I asked.

"Here's your answer," she said, walking toward me, handing me the tests. I looked at the results on all five tests, and then I looked over at her. She showed no emotion. I plopped down on the bed, sinking my head into my hands. "Candice, have a seat," I said, gesturing to the space next to me on the bed. She sat down. "What exactly do you want from me?" I asked in a calm voice. However, she remained quiet. "This is not the time for silence. We need to talk about this," I said, looking down at the five negative pregnancy tests. Still, she said nothing.

My anger had surpassed the point of yelling and throwing insults. Obviously, that wasn't working for her, anyway. Her obsession with wanting to be in my life unnerved me. "You need to say something, Candice. Because right now, it looks like you were trying to trap me with a baby that doesn't even exist."

She was trembling. "I'm sorry," she whispered.

I took several deep breaths while I tried to figure out my next move. "Okay," I said, breaking the silence. "Once you leave this room, we have nothing else to discuss. Don't contact me, don't show up anywhere you know I'll be, don't even say my name." She didn't respond, but I felt her body tense. She stood, picked up her belongings, and left the room without another word.

I had a few more hours to burn before I had to get over to the airport. I was relieved Candice wasn't pregnant, but I couldn't help thinking about my life with a family of my own. I wondered what kind of husband and father I would be or if I was even cut out for it. I laid back and eventually ended up taking a short nap. When I woke up, it was time to head over to the airport. I called an Uber and waited downstairs for it to arrive. For the first time all day, I checked my phone. *This just keeps getting better.*

The first thing I saw was the leaked photos of Candice and me from the video shoot. One photo of her rubbing my chin, the other of her dancing on me, and the icing on the cake was the photo of her licking my lips. If I saw it, then I knew Serenity had seen it. It was only then I noticed that she had never responded to my text from earlier, and she always responded to me. I had to get back home.

Chapter Twenty-Seven

Serenity.

It was well past midnight when I heard my doorbell ring. I was up. I couldn't sleep and knew who it was at my door at this hour. After all, he had called me at least twenty times since this afternoon. I uncovered myself with my blanket and crept to answer the door. I opened it to find a semi-smiling Wesley. "I hope I didn't wake you, but you didn't answer my calls, and I needed to see you tonight," he said. I allowed him entrance to my home without offering him a word. I sat back down on the couch and pulled my blanket back over me. "Do you mind if I sit?" he asked, seeming unsure of my mood.

"Sure, have a seat," I said.

"I'm guessing you saw the pictures online of Candice and me?" He held my hand and said, "Serenity, it's not what it looks like. I didn't know she would be in LA, and I didn't know she was hired to be in the video. I know it looks bad. But believe me, it's over between her and me.

I gave him a questionable look. "Does her being in LA have anything to do with you changing your flight today?" I asked.

He lowered his head and sighed, "Yes, but I can explain."

"Wesley, there's no need for you to explain. You don't owe me anything. We haven't known one another very long, and it seems like you still have some loose ends to tie up."

He leaned his head back on the couch. "I do need to explain this to you because I care about you and how you feel about me matters," he said.

He proceeded to tell me about all of the encounters he's had with Candice over the past couple of weeks. From her showing up almost naked at his house, to the video shoot and at his hotel yesterday morning claiming she was pregnant. I believed him, but this was a lot. I'd spent close to two years working on becoming the best version of me and removing drama from my life. As much as I felt like Wesley and I had a genuine connection I wanted to explore with him, he still had some work to do. "Wesley, at the bare minimum, I need to be able to trust that you'll be upfront with me. You should have told me these things were going on with Candice, instead, you hid it from me. I care about you, but I won't allow myself to be put in a position to be hurt by you. Look at this," I said, showing him Candice's posts and thumbing through the several others that accompanied it.

"If we were together, do you believe your excuses would be enough to explain this?" I showed him the picture of Candice licking him. "This may be cool in the entertainment world, and I know that's what you're used to. But I live in the real world. And in my world, things like this are an automatic dealbreaker. I already thought us dating was a stretch, and if this is the type of stuff I have to look forward to, I can't do it. I've already done this one time before, and I refuse to do it again. I think we should just not see each other right now, Wesley. This whole thing is a mess, and I need some space from it." Saying these words to him shredded my insides, but my mind had been made up. I had to protect myself.

He lowered his head again and rubbed his face with both hands. "Serenity," he whispered. "You have to know that I would never try to deliberately hurt you. You're all I want. You're all I think about. She doesn't mean anything to me." He scooted closer to me and turned my head toward him so that I could look into his eyes. "You're all I want," he repeated.

I took a deep breath. "Does she know that? If I am all you want, then this should have never happened. She should have never had a chance to get this close to you, video or not. I know we haven't decided what this is between us yet, but I am not going to do this. You and I together —" I sighed, stopping myself from exposing my insecurities.

"Wesley, I think you should go," I whispered. His eyes changed a bit after my statement. He looked at me for a moment. I guess he was hoping I would change my mind, but I couldn't. If this was just our beginning, I already knew how it would end. It was better to cut it off now. He pulled me into a hug. "I'm sorry I let this happen. I know I should have handled it better. It just happened so fast. I don't want to lose what we have going over this," he said.

My heart started to get a familiar ache of heartbreak. "Wesley, you need to sort things out with her. In her mind, she still feels like you and she have a chance to get back together. I don't care what she told you in LA. I'm a woman, and I know how she's feeling. I need you to give me some time. Just leave. Please."

After kissing my cheek and forehead, he reluctantly let me go. He stood and looked down at me for a long moment. I didn't extend him the courtesy of meeting his eyes, but I felt him. I followed the sound of his footsteps out of the door.

Chapter Twenty-Eight

Wesley.

It had been over two months since I'd last heard from or seen Serenity—seventy-one days to be exact. My heart and mind were all over the place. I kept beating myself up about how I should have handled that whole situation with Candice better. I knew I had messed up, but I had never felt so torn up over a woman before. In the short time I'd known her, Serenity had shown me how important it was to connect with someone on levels that were more than just physical. Her sweet personality and the genuine interest she showed in me as a person changed me. Her presence in my life challenged me to want to do better for her and myself. I missed her, and I was willing to do whatever it was I needed to do to get back in her life. The only problem was, she wouldn't talk to me. My calls and texts went unanswered. I sent flowers to her job and received no response. It was obvious she was moving on, but I was stuck.

I couldn't even bring myself to engage with another woman, Monica, who I called out of her bed in the middle of the night to come through. Monica showed up ready. She wore a top that barely covered her ample bare breasts and a pair of shorts that left nothing to the imagination. She didn't use any words to greet me. She began pulling down my boxers before I'd closed the front door. A few months ago, I would have been all on her, but now, all I could think about was Serenity. *Ain't this some shit?* I stopped Monica, and I felt like a complete bum trying to explain how I was no longer in the mood after she made a thirty-minute drive in the middle of the night to see me. She cursed me out before storming out of the door, slamming it behind her. I felt bad, but I realized that if I couldn't have Serenity, I didn't want anyone. I no longer had the same appetite. Serenity had given me a taste of something I'd been starving for, and I couldn't go back to things that didn't satiate me.

The song I did with Young Problem debuted at number one, partly because of his celebrity but mainly because of the drama surrounding Candice and me in the video. The director did not cut out the parts of the video I asked him to once he realized how viral the leaked pictures had become. I had no one, but myself, to blame. I knew I shouldn't have agreed to work with her because she had become too unpredictable. My Instagram following swelled to over 750,000 after the video dropped. I got messages from thousands of Xtascy fans applauding my performance and requesting a reunion album with the fellas. I started to engage more with my fans online and found things to do to keep most of my days busy. However, at the end of every day, my thoughts went right back to Serenity. She didn't post much online. I just wanted to get a peek at her. I knew I needed to do something to get myself out of this rut.

After having lunch with Pop, I went by D's shop to chop it up with him for a minute. He was in his office doing paperwork when I got there. "Yo! Best in the Wes! What up, man?" D greeted me.

"Nothing, bro. Just came from having lunch with Pops. I wanted to talk to him about a new project I'm thinking about working on," I said as I sat down.

"New project?" D asked.

"Yeah, I've been writing a lot lately, and I'm thinking about recording a new album. Just five or six songs, nothing big."

D raised his eyebrows. "She really has you in your feelings, huh?" D said, giving me a serious stare.

I leaned back in the chair and sighed, "I just miss her, man." Admitting I missed Serenity out loud felt like I was releasing pressure that had been building up in my chest.

D took a deep breath. "Look, I know Amaya wouldn't want me to tell you this, but your girl started spending time with that security guard dude, Julian, again. I don't know all the details, but I think she went out on a few dates with other guys first before they started hanging out again. I met him at Amaya's birthday party dinner a couple of weeks back. I don't know, he just seemed like he was trying too hard with her. You know?" I couldn't tell if my heart dropped to my stomach or rose to my throat after learning that information. All I know is that I couldn't respond. "I'm sorry, man," D said.

I shook my head, trying to show little emotion, but I know D felt my disappointment. "It's been over two months. I can't blame her for moving on. I should be doing the same," I said in a low tone.

"She hasn't moved on, she's just burning up time with that dude!" D said, pulling a slight smile from my injured face. "I know she was mad at you for the whole video thing, and you were wildin' for that one, bro! But she must have been hurt pretty bad to cut you off like that."

I sighed, "I don't know what else to do, short of showing up at her house and making her talk to me."

"Nah, I don't think that will work with a woman like her," D explained. "You have to show her that she can trust you. This whole thing went down with Candice, and you've never publicly cleared the air. You just let it run its course like you didn't care that it happened. She had to sit back with the rest of the world and watch Candice have her way with you. You didn't even try to put the rumors to rest. I know you want to be the good guy and don't want to make anyone look bad, but she made you look bad. You're protecting the wrong woman. It's not a good look," D said, not softening his words for me as usual.

"Look, I didn't want to fan the fire. Stories like that die out fast, and I didn't want it out there longer than it needed to be. I didn't want to give Candice any more of my energy. I wasn't trying to hurt Serenity with all of this, though, man."

"Wes, I told you in the beginning that Serenity is not like the type of woman you're used to dealing with. You need to go after her. You have to show her that you're worthy of her. She is not going to come running back to you. She has options, and according to what I hear when Amaya is talking to her, they're not just your regular dudes. These guys are lawyers, doctors, and CEOs. If you want her back, you have to put yourself out there and be willing to accept a yes or a no. With her, you have to come correct or not at all," he said and held up his hands.

"I know. She's in a class of her own. As messed up as I've been over her, I still admire that she's standing by her word. She just ain't gonna let me slide because I'm *Wesley.* She's not giving me any passes. And I'll be honest with you, that lets me know she's who I want even more."

D and I talked more about Serenity and how things were with his son and Amaya. I knew I would have to dig deep and swallow my pride a little if I wanted Serenity back in my life. I didn't care, though. I knew she was worth it. Even though I hated being apart from her, I appreciated that she stuck by her principles. Protecting her heart was her priority, and I respected that. My heart told me that she was the woman I was meant to fall in love with. I guess Pop was right about her; I chuckled at the thought. I had loved a few women in the past, but Serenity was pure love. After meeting her, I was confident I had never been *in love* with anyone before. My world did not feel as good without her. I needed to see her face, hear her laugh, and hold her close to me.

Chapter Twenty-Nine

Serenity.

I woke up in a hospital bed with monitors beeping and an IV in my arm. I felt a little dizzy. I opened my eyes to see Maya sleeping in the chair beside me. "Hey," I said.

She jolted awake. "Hey, how are you feeling?" she asked.

I'm okay, I think. What happened?"

"You passed out at work. You had me down as your emergency contact. Someone from your job called me. The doctor said you were severely dehydrated, and your blood count is a little low. She said you'll be good to leave tonight. They just wanted to monitor you for a while."

I took a cleansing breath. "I already talked to your parents, I convinced them not to come, but they want you to call them as soon as you feel up to it," Maya said.

"Thank you," I whispered.

"You're awake," I heard Julian's voice travel from the opening of the door. He carried a couple of drinks and vending machine snacks he'd gotten for him and Maya. He put the snacks down and walked over to me. "You scared me to death, Serenity. You have to take better care of yourself," he whispered, thumbing my temple.

"I'll be back, girl. I have to go to the restroom," Maya announced as she stood from her chair, taking a good stretch. Julian navigated his way around all of my cords and wires to get in the bed with me. He was holding me like it was his sole duty to protect me. "I was so worried," he said.

"I'm okay. I'm fine," I assured him.

Lately, Julian and I had been spending a lot of time together. I went out on a few dates with successful and attractive men, but their vibes weren't connecting with me. I approached Julian after work one day and asked him if he wanted to talk. We talked for a long time that night. I didn't tell him anything specific about my situation with Wesley, though I suspected he knew something had gone on between us. We began talking daily and going out, almost picking up where we left off. I told him about my decision to practice celibacy, and Julian said he didn't have an issue with it. I don't know how much I believed him, but he hadn't done anything that made me uncomfortable.

Julian often wrote me sweet poems and encouraged me to try to write some, too, after he saw my journal on my coffee table one day. He always did things to make me feel special. He even tried to cook me an iron-rich dinner when I told him about my challenges with being anemic, and it turned out okay. The fact that he even tried made me like him even more. Julian made me feel safe, and he always considered my feelings. I liked Julian, and things were going well between us.

However, I would be lying if I said I didn't still think about Wesley. Honestly, I couldn't stop thinking about him. A couple of weeks ago, Wesley posted behind the scenes footage from the video shoot for *Main Chick*. The video clip showed him storming off the set and complaining about Candice's lack of professionalism. I could also see how Candice darted away from him once the director ended the take. The clip was on Instagram and went viral for a couple of days. His caption read: *"We were never back together. We've been over for a while now, and I've moved on. This is what really happened on set that day. I chose to be professional; she chose to try and make a point. Point made. Once you're done with someone, stay done with them."* I was glad to see that he finally addressed the situation, but I wasn't sure if that was enough.

Maya and Darren were now an official couple, and I'd never seen her so happy. She and Darren were a perfect fit. They had only been together for a couple of months, and Darren had already told Maya that he loved her. I already knew it, though. I knew they had fallen for one another the first day they met at his barbershop. I would call her after work to find out she stayed over at Darren's place most nights. I was glad she was happy. Darren treated her the way she deserved to be treated. At Maya's birthday dinner a few weeks ago, I introduced Darren to Julian. He gave Julian what seemed to be a death stare for the first part of the night but loosened up a little bit once they started talking about sports. I knew Darren's loyalty was to Wesley, but he made an effort to be welcoming to Julian just to make Maya happy.

This morning, I woke up for work not feeling too great, but not bad enough to stay home, either. I only felt worse throughout the day. By one o'clock, I was making arrangements to head home and get some rest. I must have looked like a wreck by the time I made it down to the lobby of my building because Julian's smile disappeared when he saw me. "Serenity, are you okay?" he asked, holding the back of his hand to my face.

"No," I barely got out. "I'm not feeling too good. I'm heading home," I said, trying to speed past him to get to my car.

"You're burning up! You need to see a doctor."

"I just need to rest."

"No. I'm taking you to the hospital right now," he said, picking up the phone to call someone. I think I lost my balance or blacked out or something because that's the last thing I remembered.

"Serenity," I heard a familiar voice say at that same opening of the door where Julian entered minutes ago. Both Julian and I looked up to see Wesley and Darren entering the room.

"Wesley—" I called out, surprised. I hadn't seen him almost three months. My heart raced at the sight of him. He froze at the sight of Julian and me in bed together. He was visibly bothered.

"D was on the phone with Maya when she got the call that you were being taken to the hospital, and—" Wesley's eyes shifted from me to Julian and back. "I just wanted to make sure you were okay."

Julian, being the king of petty I didn't know he was, kissed me on my forehead and said, "Yeah, she's good, man. I'm taking good care of her." He carefully exited the bed, ensuring not to disturb any of my attachments. He pulled the paper-thin hospital blankets over me, leaned down to my face, and asked, "Do you need anything else, baby?" I shook my head. He kissed me once again, this time on the lips before turning around toward Wesley and Darren, who silently watched his display.

Julian took a few quick steps and extended his hand to Darren. "Nice to see you again, Darren." Darren extended his hand to Julian and shook it. Then he looked over to Wesley, extending that same hand. "Wesley, right? Good to see you again, too, man."

My eyes grew wide, but no one was paying attention to me right now. Wesley scoffed. We all knew Julian knew Wesley's name. He was just drawing his line in the sand. His demeanor said, '*You blew it, and she's mine now.*'

Wesley clenched his jaw and shook Julian's hand, gripping him tighter than I'm sure he needed to. "Yeah, it's Wesley," he finally responded. Wesley looked at me, Julian looked at Wesley, and Darren just stood there watching the tension-filled confrontation take place.

"Come on, Wes, let's go. Let her get some rest, man," Darren said, patting him on the shoulder. When they turned to leave, Maya was coming back into the room now filled with three attractive men. She determined the scene that must have played out before she entered.

"Everybody okay up in here?" she asked like she was ready to handle anyone who was bringing drama into my space.

"We're good, we were just leaving," Wesley answered.

"Okay, then," she said, pulling Darren's neck down to meet her mouth for a kiss. "I'll call you later, honey," she said.

Julian walked back over to my bedside and began stroking my hair, another unnecessary display of affection. My neat updo I started with this morning was now all over the place. Wesley turned to look at me. "Call me if you need anything, Serenity."

"I just told you, *Wesley*, I got her. She's in good hands," Julian said, now sounding annoyed.

"Julian—" I called out, trying to keep the peace because I didn't want any unnecessary drama right now.

Wesley, seemingly unphased by Julian's comment, said, "You got my number. It hasn't changed." He gave

Julian a threatening look before he and Darren left the room.

Maya returned to her chair, and Julian attempted to get back in the bed with me. "Julian, why don't you let me take it from here," Maya said. "You can go home, and I'll make sure to call you when the doctor releases her. I'll make sure she's good."

He looked at me and asked, "Is that okay with you?"

Yeah, I'm fine. You can go home. I'll call you later, okay?"

He took a minute or two to gather his things and kissed me on my cheek before leaving. Once we were sure he was gone, Maya got up to close the door. "Baby! Were they getting ready to tear up this hospital room?" We both laughed out loud. "What was Julian doing? He was like, this is my woman, my guy! You don't need to do anything for her! Back all the way up! I was here for it, though! Let me find out Julian got hands!" Maya teased. It wasn't funny, but all I could do was laugh.

"I'm just glad Wesley kept himself cool," I said. "He looked like he was ready to take Julian's head off. When he walked in, Julian was all hugged up in the bed with me. I was surprised to see him."

"I'm sorry. I'm sure Darren told him you were here. I'll talk to him about that later. But obviously, he still cares about you, or he wouldn't have come. We're going to have to get you fixed up because you can't be in a hospital bed with two men ready to throw hands over you!" she joked.

A little while later, the doctor came in to release me so I could go home. She told me to take tomorrow off from work, but I should be good to go back on my next scheduled day. It was a quarter to eight, and I was ready to go. My car was still at work. Maya said she would get someone to pick it up for me tomorrow. Right now, she just wanted to get me home.

She called my parents and Julian while I was getting dressed to tell them she was taking me home. As I was being wheeled down to the main entrance by an aide, she called Darren, too, telling him she was bringing me home. Therefore, she wouldn't be staying at his place tonight because she was staying with me. When we got to my house, I saw a familiar vehicle parked on the curb. I leaned my head back against the headrest and sighed.

Chapter Thirty

Wesley.

After D and I left Serenity's hospital room, I was burning up over seeing her and that Julian guy together. I could ignore him being petty, but I couldn't ignore how he held her, kissed her, and had his hands in her hair, right in front of me. I hated to admit it, but I was jealous it wasn't me in his place. Seeing her with him gutted me. Also, I didn't know how she ended up in the hospital in the first place. I decided not to go home. I was too unsettled and needed to make sure she was okay. A couple of hours had passed, and D called to let me know Amaya was bringing Serenity home and staying the night with her. I drove to her house and parked out front to wait for them to arrive.

Amaya parked in Serenity's driveway and exited her vehicle. She walked up to my driver's side window before I could even get the door open. "Hi, Wesley, what's up?" she asked, resting her hands on the roof of the car.

"I just want to talk to her, Amaya. I want to make sure she's okay." She turned her head, looking back at her parked vehicle where Serenity still sat.

"Alright, Wesley. I'm on your side, but don't do or say anything that will make me regret this," she said with a slight smile.

"Okay," I agreed. I rolled up the window and got out of my truck. I walked with Amaya to the passenger side door of her car.

"You can get her; I'll get the front door," she instructed. I opened the door and peered down at the only woman who made my heart skip a beat by just looking at me. When she looked up at me, I knew I couldn't go another day without her. I wouldn't. We didn't speak; I just offered her my hand.

By this time, Amaya had made it to the front door and was inside the house already. Serenity took my hand and let me help her up. Even though she had just been through a whole ordeal, and I hadn't seen her in close to three months at this point, the sight of her face still activated the butterflies in my stomach. "Thank you," she whispered.

I cleared my throat and said, "I wanted to make sure you were okay. What happened? How did you end up in the hospital?" I didn't want to overwhelm her, but I needed answers.

"I passed out at work, and Julian drove me to the hospital."

"He drove you? Why didn't he call an ambulance?" I asked, trying to remain calm. I took a breath, realizing I was getting ready to fly off the handle at the sound of his name.

"I'm anemic. The doctor said I was dehydrated, and my blood count was low. I didn't feel well this morning, but I went to work anyway. I'm glad I did. If I had stayed home, I could have passed out without anyone knowing. Julian stopped me from driving home. I'm glad he was there."

As much as I wanted to not like this guy, I was glad he was there to get her the medical attention she needed. "I'm just glad you're okay," I said.

"I am, and thank you for coming by."

"So, you and Julian …" I trailed off because I felt stupid even attempting to ask.

"I'm sorry about earlier. He shouldn't have acted like that," she said, looking embarrassed.

"You don't need to apologize; I understand." I paused to look at her hand that I was still holding. "So, are you and him … together? At least, that's how it looked to me."

She dropped her eyes to the ground. "We've been seeing one another, but we're not a couple." That statement gave me a tiny pinch of relief. "Well, I need to go inside to change and relax. I'm a little tired. Thank you again for coming by and checking on me, Wesley."

She let go of my hand and began walking up the driveway toward her front door. I grew more anxious with every step she took in the opposite direction. I didn't know what to say, but I wasn't just going to let her leave. I opened my mouth to speak when Amaya came back outside and said, "Wesley! Would you mind sitting with her until I get back? I need to go pick up a few things from the store really quick."

I picked up my feet to walk Serenity inside. "Yeah, no problem," I said, giving Amaya a look of appreciation. She acknowledged me back with her eyes before darting into her car and backing out the driveway.

Once we were inside alone, we stood facing one another, not knowing what to say. "Well, you can have a seat in the living room. I'm going to change out of these clothes," she said.

I grabbed her arm when she turned to walk away, "I'm sorry for what happened with Candice. I know what I did hurt you. I know I have to earn your trust, but I'm willing to put in the work. I've missed you, Serenity. It's been months. I've given you time and space because that's what you said you needed. But I need you," I said, lifting her chin with my finger so I could look into her eyes. "I'm sorry I ever made you doubt me. Can you please forgive me?" I asked, not caring if I sounded like I was teetering on the line of begging.

She looked up at me on the verge of tears. "Wesley, I can't trust that you'll be upfront with me. And if I can't trust you, I can't be with you," she murmured as tears began to fall. "It's more than just the video. Every woman I've seen you with has looked like they walked straight off the runway and into your life. That's a different world. I don't look like those women, and whatever it is they have that you want, I can't give to you. I miss you, too, but I can't let you hurt me. I won't go through that again."

She began to walk away. Her words hit me like Muhammed Ali in his prime, giving me a body shot. I realized I spread an insecurity in her that I hadn't known was there to begin with. Seeing the pain on her face and hearing the regret in her voice made me feel disappointed in myself. I never wanted her to feel like I was out of her league. Truth be told, I felt like I was out of hers. I pulled her into a hug from behind, holding her with one arm across her waist and the other one across her chest, gripping her shoulder. She dropped her head and I buried my face in her hair, before moving to plant soft kisses on her neck. "You're beautiful inside and out. No one from my past measures up to what you've already given me. You got them all beat, and I can't stop thinking about you. You're who I want. I can't go another day without you. The shit hurts too bad," I whispered into her ear. I now pleaded with her, because I wasn't losing this woman without a fight. I calmed in the vibration of her heartbeat against my forearm.

She broke free from my embrace and turned to face me. Her eyes met mine with more tears threatening to fall.

"Wesley, I —"

I broke her sentence by kissing her. I took in her lips, and my tongue was granted instant access to her mouth. I groaned at the taste and feel of her. My restraint, that was already holding on by a thread, broke without warning. I couldn't stop myself from ravaging her at this moment. My hands were all over her; I couldn't hold back my desire. This had to be all in my imagination, but I wasn't taking any chances just in case it wasn't. I lifted her light frame, all 130 pounds of her, up by her legs and pressed her back against the front door. She wrapped her legs around my waist, and the kisses we shared grew more passionate.

"I'm so sorry I hurt you. I'll apologize as many times as it takes until you forgive me. Will you forgive me?" I asked, returning to our heated exchange.

She whimpered. I began to trail kisses down her neck to the middle of her chest. She gripped the back of my neck and rubbed her hands in my hair. I began sucking and licking her neck. I felt the heat between her legs rise as I held her captive between the door and me.

I paused for a moment to catch my breath. I knew I would have rather played in traffic on a freeway instead of saying what I was about to say. "Serenity, as much as I want you right now, and I'm sure you can feel how much I want you right now, we should probably stop."

I did not recognize the man saying that. Who had I become? What was I doing? I knew she had boundaries. I didn't want her to regret doing anything with me. I knew I could have sex with any woman I desired, but I wanted her and me to make love one day. And this wasn't it. We embraced each other, racing to slow down our breathing.

"You're right. I'm sorry," she whispered, her breaths tickling my ear.

"Please, don't be sorry!" I chuckled. "I just know you don't want it like this, and I want to give you what you want. I want to do this right with you. I need you to trust me. Do you think I can earn your trust back?"

She looked at me with her arms still wrapped around my neck. "Yes, Wesley. You can, but that was your only strike with me. Next time, you're out."

"There won't be a next time," I responded. We kissed again. This time, it was much gentler. I placed her on her feet. I sat on the couch while she went to change.

✳ ✳ ✳ ✳ ✳

When Amaya came back from the store, Serenity and I were seated on the couch, watching TV, looking comfortable together. We sat next to each other and shared a blanket, but we didn't allude to what transpired earlier. She came in carrying a few bags.

"Let me help you," I offered.

"Thank you. I know it's a little late to eat dinner. But I'm hungry, and I know Renny hasn't eaten anything since earlier. There's enough here for you, too, Wesley, if you want to stick around," Amaya said, unpacking cartons of food on the counter. She made a plate for Serenity and motioned for me to take it to her. I liked Amaya more and more. She was a good friend to Serenity, and when Amaya said she was on my side, she meant it. She followed behind me, carrying two plates, one for herself and one for me.

I had to get the name of the Chinese food place Amaya went to because that food was on hit! Serenity didn't eat much off of her plate, so I found myself trying to feed her some broccoli. Amaya gave us a questionable but approving look. It was hard to keep my hands to myself after being apart from Serenity for almost three months, but

I did. I'm sure our flirtatious behavior wasn't lost to Amaya, who watched TV and scrolled through her phone. Serenity leaned her head on my chest, and I rested my arm around her. Her presence soothed me, and the rhythm of her breathing sounded like the softest melody. I knew more than anything that I wanted to be the man for her. I also knew I had put her in an awkward position with Julian by my actions earlier, but she assured me she could handle the conversation with him.

The doorbell rang, and I looked at my watch. "Are you expecting someone this late?" I asked Serenity, showing a look of concern.

"I got it," Amaya said, jumping up. "It's just Darren. He's bringing me the overnight bag I left at his house."

Darren walked around the corner with Amaya, holding her little duffle bag. "Hey, Ren, how are you feeling, sweetheart?"

"I feel okay," she answered, giving D a pleasant smile.

"Good, I'm glad you're feeling better." Then he looked at me and changed the tone of his voice. "When I pulled up to this address and saw a black Range Rover parked out front, I thought to myself, I have to have the wrong address because I know that's not Wes' truck out here this late! And look, here you are! All snuggled up!" We all laughed. Serenity offered D a seat, and Amaya made him a plate.

We all sat and talked like we were old friends. "All I'm saying is the red hair was not your best look in that video for "Summer Girl!" Serenity laughed, with Amaya and D joining in with her.

"What are you talking about? My hair was dope! You couldn't tell me nothing! D, you're the one who did it, and you're laughing, bro?" I said, unable to help myself from laughing, too.

"I tried to talk you out of it, but you didn't want to listen! I just gave you what you asked for!" D recalled.

"It's okay, Wesley. You still looked good," Serenity said, silencing the room with a sweet tone and the look she gave me.

I wanted to kiss her but said, "Thank you," instead, holding her gaze.

D looked at us and blurted, "Do y'all need some privacy?" That speaking without thinking first characteristic of his was his blessing and curse.

Amaya nudged him.

"What?" he asked, not seeing anything wrong with the question.

"It's pretty late. It's time for you two to head home," Amaya said in a sleepy voice. Amaya and D stood up and walked over to the front door to say their goodbyes in private.

I grasped Serenity's hand and toyed with her hospital bracelet. "I need you to take care of yourself, okay?" I kissed her hand. "I'll be back over tomorrow to check on you. I'll call you." I gave her a quick kiss on the cheek, and then I joined D outside.

D and I leaned against my truck. He looked over at me, holding his chin between his index finger and thumb. "You good, man?" he asked.

My smile gave it away. "Yeah," I answered, looking up at Serenity's house with a smile I had no intention of hiding. "I'm good," I said, pushing my back off my truck and extending my arm for the standard gentleman's handshake.

"She's a good woman. Don't mess that up again!" was D's only advice. We said our goodbyes for the night and drove our separate ways.

Chapter Thirty-One

Serenity.

The next morning, I had text messages waiting from Wesley and Julian, checking to see how I felt. I told Maya what happened between Wesley and me last night when she went to the store.

She squealed. "So, you two are good now?" she asked.

"We are. We do need to talk a little bit more. But Maya, every time I see him or hear his voice, it's like my heart smiles. It's a feeling I've never had before. I can't ignore that."

"Awe, Renny! You light up when you're around him. He does, too. Even Ray Charles can see the chemistry between y'all!" she joked.

"I just have to talk to Julian," I sighed. "I hate to do this to him again, but I'm not going to string him along."

"Julian will be just fine, believe me. His feelings may be a little hurt. But if he truly cares about you, he'll want you to do what makes you happy. If you really feel that giving Wesley another chance will make you happy, then that's what you should do. Just make sure it's what you truly want."

Maya and I turned the rest of our morning into gossiping, laughing, and catching up on some reality TV shows I had recorded. She wasn't the type of friend who would allow me to stay sick or down for long. Her energy was always positive, and it was contagious.

After making sure I had everything I needed, Maya left my house around one o'clock. Julian would be coming over after work to check in on me. That was fine. I knew I needed to talk to him sooner than later. As much as I liked him, I knew anything more with him wouldn't be right. Wesley said he'd be over around six o'clock tonight.

Julian arrived at my house soon after his shift. He greeted me with a hug and a kiss on my cheek. "You look like you're feeling better," he remarked.

"I am." He followed me into the kitchen, where I poured each of us a double shot of brown liquor. He sat behind the counter while I played bartender. I gave him a look of regret, "Julian —"

"I already know, Serenity, you don't have to tell me," he said, stopping me. I gave him a curious look.

"You're not over that Wesley guy, right?" he asked, gulping down his drink. "I saw the way you two looked at each other yesterday at the hospital, and you don't look at me like that."

"I'm sorry," I said, feeling guilty because I was a little relieved. "I hope you're not mad, Julian. I think you're a beautiful man with an amazing heart, and you deserve someone who will return your love completely. You deserve that. I want that for you," I said, taking a sip of my drink.

"Thank you, and I think you're a gorgeous woman with an amazing heart, and you deserve happiness, too," he said, putting his glass down and walking over to me. He stood in front of me, my back to the counter, gazing down at me like he was a lion and I was his fresh kill. He had an easy way of making me emotionally submit to him that I couldn't explain or deny. He held me by my arms, "Serenity, I love you," he confessed for the first time. "I'll always love you regardless of whether or not we're together. I want you to be happy. I wish I could flip a switch and make myself be the man for you, but I can't. I see it in your eyes. You're there, but you won't fully let me in," he said, making me widen my eyes a bit. "Why won't you let me in?" he asked in a whisper, leaning in to kiss me.

I moved my face from his advance. "Julian ..." He lifted me to a sitting position on the counter, placing his hands on both sides of me, and leaned in close to my face. "I want to give you all that you want."

He gently rubbed the back of his hand on my cheek. "The ways I've dreamed of pleasuring you ..." he licked his bottom lip. "Pleasuring all of you. I want to know what you feel like, Serenity. I want the taste of you on my lips. Is that so wrong?" he whispered. My body temperature spiked from his words alone. *Why was he doing this to me?* Julian may not have been who I felt in my heart, but I am still a woman who hadn't been with a man in quite a while. It didn't take much to turn on those bedroom thoughts, and Julian's energy right now had the potential to make me throw caution to the wind.

"Julian, please, don't make this harder than it needs to be." I muscled up the will to say. He was inches away from my face and his eyes begged me to submit. "Julian, I can't." I nudged him away from me and hopped down from the counter. "Come on, let me walk you out." I held him by the wrist and led him to the front door. He hugged me, holding his head in the nook of my neck. His embrace told me that he didn't want to let me go, but he knew he had to. He squeezed his fingertips into my back and gave me a parting kiss on my forehead.

"I'll always be here for you, Serenity. You're God's gift to me."

I didn't have anything to say, so I just nodded. I opened the door for him to leave. Our eyes locked, and the silent acknowledgment of the end of our journey washed over us. I closed the door behind him.

$$*****$$

Before Wesley arrived, I talked to my parents for about a half-an-hour. When I opened the door for him, he had several bags full of food. "What's all of this?" I asked.

"Just a few things I picked up that I thought you might like." I reached over to pick up a bag to help him. "I got this; you just have a seat and let me spoil you for the rest of the night," he said, giving me a soft kiss on the lips.

"Okay, I'm not going to argue!" I said, heading back over to the couch and getting comfy with my fleece blanket. I had plenty of shows to catch up on.

He walked over to the kitchen, emptied the groceries on the counter, and began preparing us dinner. He asked me where I kept a few of my kitchen items. But for the most part, he allowed me to rest and watch my shows. I heard him humming melodies to himself while he cooked. I also saw him taking a few pictures of his creation. I can't lie—whatever he was making smelled great, and it was making me hungry.

"Are you ready to eat?" he asked from the kitchen. I looked over to see him wearing a full apron, a kitchen towel laying over his shoulder, and a smile that said he was, no doubt, proud of himself.

"Yes, I'm ready. Everything smells delicious!" He brought me a plate that looked so good that I would have bet it came from a five-star restaurant. If he hadn't made it in my kitchen, I would have thought he paid someone to make it.

"Oh, my goodness! Wesley, how did you learn how to do this?"

"After our cooking class, I started watching a lot of cooking videos. Then I started watching the Food Channel, and I saw some things I wanted to try making. I had a lot of failures. But I needed to stay busy, and cooking was like therapy for me."

I smiled. "Well, I'm impressed! Can you tell me what we're having?"

"Yes! This is chicken with potatoes and chives, braised in a white wine and butter sauce, served with roasted lemon pepper asparagus, sprinkled with olive oil and parmesan cheese."

"This looks incredible, Wesley!" We held hands while he prayed over our food. When I took the first bite, I wanted to melt! Everything was cooked and seasoned perfectly. He just had a natural talent for developing flavors. His food tasted like he'd been cooking for years.

"I'm glad you like it," he said, with an impossibly handsome grin.

Chapter Thirty-Two

***Wesley*.**
I cleared our plates and finished cleaning up the kitchen while Serenity and I held a conversation from across the room. I sat with her and began watching whatever she had on the TV. I didn't care what was on; I just wanted to be next to her. "Put your feet up here," I said, patting my hands on my lap. I took off her socks and started massaging her pretty little feet. My hands were big enough to almost cover her whole foot. "How does that feel?" I asked.

She moaned. "It feels good! You're just a jack of all trades, huh? You sing, cook, clean, and give massages," she joked.

I laughed. "I just want you to feel better. Seeing you in that hospital bed yesterday scared me. Whatever I can do for that not to happen again, I'll do."

"Thank you, Wesley. I'll take better care of myself. I don't want something like that to happen again, either."

"How did your conversation with Julian go today?" I asked, not really wanting to bring it up, but needing to know.

"He stopped by after work earlier, so we could talk. He had already figured you and I still had something going on between us when you came to the hospital," she sighed. "But it was fine. He took the news okay."

"What did he say?"

"He said a few things. Basically, he told me that he wants me to be happy."

I scoffed. "And that he'll be there for you if you ever need him, right?" I added.

She looked over to me, confirming what I already knew. "Yeah, but I don't need him. I have you, right?" she replied.

"You have me. I just know dudes like him. He'll fall back for a little while and play the friend card, but he'll be back. Believe me." I lifted her leg to kiss the top of her foot. "Seeing him with you yesterday at the hospital was… hard for me. Watching him kiss you and comforting you in your time of need—I couldn't handle it. I want to be that for you. I want to be the one you call on for whatever you need," I said, laying my cards on the table. "How do you feel about me? About us?"

"I feel good about you, and I feel good about us, too," she answered without faltering. "Why do you ask?"

"Well, I feel like I can be myself around you. Like, I can let my guard down. I've never been able to be just plain Wesley around any woman I've dated. I've always felt like they expected me to be some unrealistic guy who just wants to sing and buy them expensive gifts. You're not like that, though. You appreciate just spending time with me. Just me being me was good enough for you. I thought about you every day and every night after the Candice situation. Not seeing you or talking to you for this long has been torture. I was wrong. I handled that all wrong. I should have told you what was going on. I just didn't want to risk losing you because no one had ever made me feel the way you make me feel. You're special, Serenity, and I want to spend my time getting to know you better if you want to get to know me, too."

I gave her a moment to respond, still gently massaging her feet. "I would like that, Wesley," she answered, with a radiant smile.

"Oh, yeah?" I asked, smiling back.

She nodded. "Just so we're clear," I continued, "I want you all to myself. I'm all in this thing with you, and I want to do things right. I know you have a few brothas standing in line, waiting to shoot their shot. I've done my research, but I want you to myself. I feel selfish when it comes to you."

She moved her feet from my lap and got on her knees, inching herself closer to me. I grabbed her by the waist and sat her across my lap. The sudden movement made her giggle. "Wesley Johnson, are you asking me to be your girlfriend?" She asked with the sweetest smile.

Her question made me feel like the young boy who finally got the courage to ask out Sierra Thompson in the eighth grade, just for her to tell me no. I chuckled, "I'm asking you to be my woman… exclusively."

She laughed. "I'm all in this thing with you, too."

I kissed her, looking into her eyes as I withdrew from her soft full lips. We both smiled. She gave me another quick peck on the lips and repositioned herself on my chest so we could finish watching the show.

✳✳✳✳✳

It was after midnight and Serenity had me fully invested in one of her favorite reality TV shows. I wanted to see the next episode more than she did! "I can't believe she talked to her mom like that!" Serenity commented after the last episode ended. "My mom would have slapped the fire from me!"

I laughed. "You know it doesn't go down like that in Black households!" I rubbed her arm and kissed her wherever my lips fell. I'd never wanted to kiss a woman as much as I wanted to kiss her. Her lips were addictive.

"Wesley, can I ask you something?"

"Anything," I replied.

"How come you don't talk about your mother?" she asked with hesitation.

My heart felt as heavy as bricks from that question. She looked up at me, studying my eyes that I'm sure had gone blank. My mother was a subject I didn't talk about with anyone, not even with my dad.

"I'm sorry. I didn't mean to upset you," she said, straddling me and rubbing my cheek with her soft hand. She then wrapped her arms around my neck, leaning in to hug me. "I'm sorry, Wesley. We don't have to talk about it. Okay?"

I wrapped my arms around her, returning her embrace, blinking tears from my eyes. "No, it's okay," I said, taking a deep breath. "My mother died when I was nine years old. She was six months pregnant with my little brother. I was in school, and my dad was on the road touring. I was really into basketball at one point, so I kept begging her to buy me a new basketball. Every day I asked her about it. I wouldn't let up! So, one day Mom decided she would buy me one before coming to pick me up from school. She wanted to surprise me." I took another deep breath, and Serenity's eyes were fixed on me. "She got into a car accident on her way from the store. She and my unborn brother died on the scene. When my dad came home, the police gave him her belongings from the car. She had a new basketball still in the bag and a card that read, *To my sweet, Wesley. I'll be there when you make it to the NBA! Aim high, baby boy! Mommy loves you.* I recalled, with my voice struggling to keep my voice even.

"I blamed myself for their deaths for years. I thought my father blamed me too, because if I hadn't asked for it —" I said, unable to hold back my silent tears anymore. She wrapped her arms back around me, and my tears ran onto her shoulder. I held her as if she would float away if I let her go.

"It's okay, Wesley. It's okay. I got you. I'm here. It wasn't your fault," she whispered. I hadn't cried over the loss of my mother in a long time. It was one of those memories I kept locked away and kept buried. With Serenity, I felt safe being vulnerable. I didn't feel like she would look at me funny afterward or think I was any less of a man. I knew my tears were safe with her. I knew my heart was safe with her, too.

She held onto me for as long as I needed her, allowing me to feel and be anything I needed to feel and be in that moment, which felt like a luxury. She kissed my tears and wiped my eyes. She was a nurturer. I realized that had been something I'd been lacking. Normally, the women I dated didn't want to give intimacy to me like this, they just wanted to take. I would never be able to shed tears in front of anyone else like this without being judged. Serenity poured into me. She always gave first without being asked to. It was in her nature, and I appreciated it. We laid on the couch until sleep found us. I woke up at 3:00 a.m. to head home. I laid Serenity in her bed and kissed her before leaving. I didn't know what lay ahead. But as long as I had Serenity by my side, I knew every step would be worth it.

Chapter Thirty-Three

Serenity. Eight Months Later.

It was my thirty-third birthday this week, and Maya, along with the help of Wesley, had planned a party for me. It was nothing too big, just a nice dinner with friends, family, and a few co-workers. Over the last several months, my relationship with Wesley had blossomed into a love I never knew I could feel. We encouraged one another, prayed together, had long insightful conversations, and gave one another space when needed. I felt completely comfortable being myself around him. We knew how important it was for us to remain active participants in our own separate lives and nurture our individual interests.

We faced some hurdles, of course, but we always worked out our differences by communicating through love, respect, and understanding. We made a conscious effort to always be transparent with one another. Also, we took time out at least two to three times a month to talk about where we were mentally, spiritually, emotionally, and physically, within ourselves and as a unit. I truly believe this is what helped make our relationship grow strong and healthy.

One of the challenges we faced as our relationship progressed, was my vow of celibacy. Wesley never pressured me to change my mind or made me feel like he didn't support my decision. We talked extensively about my reasons for abstaining, and he gained a deeper understanding of my views of intimacy. Although I know how difficult it was for him at times, he wanted me to feel comfortable. It wasn't easy for me, either, because I wanted him just as much as he wanted me, if not more. I showed him intimacy through my words and actions. I often wrote him love notes, cooked him dinner, encouraged him to set new goals, and remained a shoulder he could always depend on. We also cuddled quite often, shared kisses, and held hands in public. Our relationship had been somewhat documented online, but we kept what would we could private. Wesley made my heart feel safe. As our love grew, it filled me.

Being with Wesley felt right. I didn't have to force anything with him. Our relationship grew naturally, and I never had to question how he felt about me. He regularly showered me with uplifting words, encouragement, and compliments. He always made me feel like the most beautiful woman in the world. He was extremely affectionate which is something I wasn't accustomed to, but I learned to appreciate.

We had been dating for three months when he rented out one of my favorite jazz clubs so we could enjoy a private night of music, dancing, and soul food. The night was going well; I couldn't have asked for anything more perfect. Wesley gifted me with a diamond tennis bracelet, along with three dozen white long-stem roses to celebrate our three-month anniversary earlier in the evening, which left me speechless. We were slow dancing to "A Sentimental Mood" by John Coltrane & Duke Ellington. Every time I looked up at his handsome face, my heart fluttered.

"Serenity, there's been something I've been wanting to tell you," he said, as the saxophonist played in time to the beat of my heart.

"Yes, Wesley?" He looked nervous.

"Every morning when I wake up, you're the first thought on my mind. I can't start my day without talking to you or scrolling through my phone to see a picture of your face. It's like, you give me permission to breathe, or something. I know I probably sound crazy, and maybe I'm not describing it right, but I've never felt anything like what I feel for you for anyone else. I've cared deeply for a few women in my past; I've even loved a couple. But I've never been *in* love before. What I'm trying to say is … I love you. I'm *in love* with you, Serenity." His eyes stayed on mine, as he still swayed me to the music.

I let out a calming sigh as my heart stalled and raced simultaneously. "I'm in love with you, too, Wesley David Johnson Jr.," I whispered, doing my best not to get my words stuck in my throat. He smiled.

"The full government, huh?" he chuckled.

I stood on my toes to kiss him. "Yup," I then returned my head to his chest to finish our dance.

❋ ❋ ❋ ❋ ❋

My parents, Beverly and Eldridge James, Jr., along with my younger brother, Eldridge the third, or Tré, were in town for the party. My brother stayed with me, but my parents opted to stay in a hotel so the visit would feel like a getaway. At least that's what they told me. I told Wesley I would arrive with my family, and he agreed to meet us there. When we arrived, everyone began to applaud. Wesley found his way over to us. "Mom, Dad, this is Wesley," I said, introducing them to a smiling and handsome Wesley. He sure did look extra fine anytime he wore a suit. Wesley had talked to my parents over the phone before, but this was their first in-person meeting. I had no idea where my brother ran off to. He greeted my mom first. "Mrs. James, it's a pleasure to meet you," he said as he gave her a friendly hug.

My mom smiled. "Nice to meet you, Wesley."

"Mr. James," he said, extending his right hand and looking my dad in his eyes. "It's good to meet you, sir."

My dad gave him a firm handshake while sizing him up. "Good to meet you, too," Dad finally said.

Just then, Maya popped up. "Mr. and Mrs. James! It's so good to see you!" she said, giving them hugs.

Then out of nowhere, my brother, Tré, appeared. "It's nice to see you again, Amaya. You look very nice," Tré said, trying to be smooth.

"Hi, Tré! Look at you! I see you're a grown man now! How old are you? Twenty-three? Twenty-four?" she asked.

He cleared his throat. "I'm twenty-five now," he said, exuding an air of confidence we all found amusing but didn't dare laugh.

"Well, I'm glad you were able to make it, Tré," she said, turning back to us. "The food is ready, and a bar is open! So, please, help yourselves."

"Mr. James, Tré, would you like to go get a drink?" Wesley asked. They agreed and began to walk over to the bar. Wesley stayed a few steps behind. "Serenity, you look stunning tonight," he said, kissing me on the cheek before catching up with my family.

My mom turned her head to look at me. "Yeah, I see what you were talking about," she said with a smirk.

The party was going well. The DJ was playing all my favorite songs, drinks were being poured, and laughter and dancing were in abundance. We had a small group of about twenty-five to thirty people in attendance, along with a few servers and a photographer. I was happy to have the people I loved most under one roof. I couldn't remember ever being this happy, but here I was. After failed relationships, diminished self-worth, and at one time feeling like I would never be able to love again, I now had the love of my life in Wesley.

Chapter Thirty-Four

Wesley.
I had to hold back my reaction when I first saw Serenity walk into the party because she was with her family. As far as I was concerned, she was always the most beautiful woman in the room. But tonight, my eyes were stuck to her like glue. She wore an emerald green, V-neck, spaghetti strapped dress that fell right above her knees and fitted her like a glove. Her long natural hair was side-parted and flowing wildly in that wavy texture I like; I think it's called a twist out. She had matching nude fingernails and toes with a pair of gold open-toe heels. Her skin looked like she had been dipped in the depths of the moon from the way she glowed. And this was all before I looked at her face. I loved that she didn't wear heavy makeup. She had on green and gold eyeshadow to match her outfit. Her lips were glossy, and her lashes looked a little fuller, but it didn't look like she had on anything else. She was flawless. I felt like the luckiest man in the world.

I enjoyed meeting her family, and I could see where Serenity got her looks from. Her mom was petite, too, and looked like a slightly older, but just as gorgeous, version of Serenity. Her dad was around my height but about thirty pounds heavier than me. Serenity said her dad used to be an amateur boxer before he opened up his own fitness gym. Judging from his build, I'm sure he was still able to put in some work in the ring.

"My baby girl seems happy with you," Mr. James said while twirling his glass of Bourbon.

"I love your daughter very much, Mr. James. My goal is to keep her happy. I want to keep that smile on her face for as long as she'll let me." I wasn't interested in playing word games. I wanted him to know I was serious about protecting his daughter's heart.

"That's good to know," he said, taking a sip. "Do you know what they called me back in the day when I used to box?" he asked, with a semi-serious look on his face.

I eyed him back. "No, sir. What did they call you?" I asked, knowing he was testing my courage.

He looked over at his smiling daughter and wife, mingling with the other partygoers. "As long as my daughter looks like that, you'll never find out," he answered, patting me on the shoulder. He held eye contact with me for a long moment and then began to laugh.

"Pop! Chill!" Tré said. "He's been using that same line since she was in high school, man. Don't even worry about it!"

"Wesley," Mr. James said, "I know you love my daughter, and I'm confident you'll do everything in your power to make sure she's good. This is the first time I didn't have to worry about who she was with and how they treated her. I know you're a good man, but I had to bust your chops a little." I smiled. But I knew deep down that he would put me to sleep over his daughter if he had to.

Pop and D also came out to the party. I had a chance to introduce them to Serenity's family. My dad was gracious, as always, and took pictures with them. Dinner was served, the gift table was full, and it was time to sing happy birthday. Of course, we had to sing the Stevie Wonder version because that was the only version I recognized. The majority of the party requested that Dad and I sing happy birthday together. I loved singing with Dad. He taught me everything I knew about how to master my vocal range. Amaya, being the professional she is, had two cordless microphones on standby, ready to go. We stood before Serenity and sang as Amaya wheeled out the cake. By the end of the song, I stood Serenity to her feet and wiped away a few tears that had fallen. She squeezed me and whispered, "I love you so much," in my ear. Everyone applauded, and I couldn't help but kiss her.

"I love you, too, baby."

"Let's dance!" Amaya said, pulling my date away from me. "I'll bring her back to you, Wesley! Don't worry!" she said, smiling at me.

"So, are you ready to do this, man?" D asked, standing next to me while we watched Serenity and Amaya dance. They had kicked off their shoes and were turnt all the way up! There were several people on the floor dancing, too.

"I am. I already got her parents' blessing last week." I looked at him. "She's the one. I've never been this sure about anything."

"Okay, bro, I got you," he assured me. Although I was confident in what I was about to do, I was still nervous. I went to the bar and got a shot of tequila.

Pop came over and sensed my nervous energy. "You'll be fine, Son," he said, patting me on the back. "Go ahead." I took a deep breath and went up to the DJ booth to grab a microphone.

The DJ lowered the music. "Can I have everyone's attention, please?" I asked. The room started to quiet down. "First, I want to thank everyone for coming out tonight to celebrate Serenity. I hope everyone is having a good time." I saw Serenity's eyes on me, and her smile melted away any nervousness I felt. "I wanted to do something special for her tonight. So, if y'all don't mind, I would like to sing a song I wrote for her." Everyone applauded. D brought up a chair to where I was standing and then escorted Serenity to sit down. She was still barefoot, smiling, and as pretty as ever. The DJ played the music track I had queued up. I began to sing:

Baby, I'll love you this way forever,
Never will our hearts not beat as one.
My life was not complete until I met you.
Forever you, forever me, forever one.
Your love is like an ocean, deep and strong.
I'd swim through any depths to feel your touch.
Baby, wash me over again and again with your currents.
Forever you, forever me, it's not too much.
The love we share is more than I had prayed for,
My heart could not go on without your love.
I thank the God above He sent you to me.
Forever you, forever me, forever us.
Your face is like the sun; I count my blessings.
Your smile, your soul, your heart, that's one, two, three.
The joy you bring my life is overflowing.
Forever us, forever you, forever me.
I pray each day to always make you happy.
You're all I want; you're all I need in my life.
I now know how true love can make me happy.
Serenity, will you be my wife?
I dropped down to one knee and held her hand. I put down the microphone and pulled a black velvet ring box out of my pocket, presenting her with a simple emerald cut, five-carat diamond ring with a diamond-studded platinum band.

"Serenity, I love you so much. You're the best thing that's ever happened to me. I never knew love could feel so good before I met you. I don't ever want to lose you. You have my heart, baby. And if it's okay with you, I want to spend the rest of my life loving you. Will you do me the honor of being my wife?"

Tears streamed down her face, and her hand trembled. All of our friends and family applauded and whistled, but I couldn't make another move until I got her answer. My eyes were fixated on the woman I wanted to be mine for the rest of my days. "Yes," she whispered.

"Yes?!" I repeated.

"Yes!" she yelled. The cheering became even louder. I slid the ring on her finger, sealing our future together. I stood, picking her up with me and kissing her the way I wanted to. I put her down and hugged her tightly. The longer I held her, the more I felt tears welling in my eyes. Amaya and Mrs. James were the first ones at Serenity's side to congratulate us. My Pop, D, and Mr. James followed. The room was full of excitement and love. I felt like I had an out-of-body experience, in a good way, though.

Last year, around this time, marriage wasn't even a possibility for me. Now, I was asking the woman I had fallen in love with to marry me. The way my life had completely changed for the better since I'd met Serenity, shocked me. I picked up the microphone one more time, still holding my new fiancé's hand. I turned to her. "I have one more gift for you, baby," I said as D gave me a small box.

"I don't think I can take anymore!" she said, making the crowd laugh.

"You'll like this, trust me." I handed her the box. "Now, before you open it, just remember, I got it on sale, so you can't take it back!" I joked, referring to her always sensible spending habits. I put the microphone down, and we all watched her open the box.

She looked up at me. "Wesley! You didn't!" She pulled out a key fob for a brand-new Mercedes Benz G

Wagon. I'd heard her make mention of how much she liked the truck before, but I knew she would never spend that much money on a car.

"It's outside waiting for you. Happy birthday, baby." I leaned over for another kiss. We all went outside to look at the brand new, midnight blue truck with a big red bow on the top. Her happiness and joy were infectious, and in turn, made me even more ecstatic to be able to add to her happiness.

It was time for people to start heading home. We thanked everyone for coming and received several congratulatory wishes on our engagement. That ring looked good on her hand, and she seemed to love showing it off. "I'm proud of you, Son," Pop said, giving me a firm hug and wiping his eyes as he stepped away.

"Serenity, welcome to the family, darling," he said, giving her an equally firm hug.

Mr. and Mrs. James and Tré wouldn't be going back to Virginia until Monday morning. I planned to have them over to my house for an early dinner tomorrow. D helped me pack up all of her gifts into my truck, and I followed her home while Tré
drove her old car behind us. I stopped behind her at a red light. All I could think was, *There goes my future wife*.

Chapter Thirty-Five

Serenity.

Tré helped Wesley bring my gifts into the house. I kept looking down at my hand. I couldn't believe I was getting married. And to the literal man of my dreams, no less! Once everything was in the house, Wesley and I finally had a moment alone to enjoy our engagement. I wrapped my arms around his neck. "Today has to be one of the happiest days of my life. Thank you, Wesley. I love you."

"I love you, too," he said, connecting his lips with mine so softly that I felt as if I could float away.

"The truck rides so smoothly. I can't believe you bought it for me! The party was more than enough. Thank you." I kissed him again.

"You're welcome, Miss James, soon to be Mrs. Johnson," he said, holding me tighter and kissing my forehead.

"Let me ask you something. If I would have said no, would you have still given me the truck?" I asked with a huge smile.

He laughed. "If you would have said no—" I stopped his sentence with a kiss. A strong one. A passionate one, pulling a groan from his mouth.

"I can go stay at the hotel if y'all need some privacy tonight!" My little brother interrupted. "I mean, I understand. Y'all are in love; you just got engaged, and you probably want to celebrate tonight," he said, making a weird face.

"Boy! Get outta here!" I yelled, throwing a pillow from my couch at him.

"See, Wesley! She's violent! Are you sure you want to marry that?" he joked.

Wesley chuckled. "I'm sure, man." He looked at me and said, "I'm going to get out of here. I have a long drive home. I'll call you when I get there. Will you wait up for me?"

"Absolutely," I answered.

"Tré, I'll see you tomorrow, man." With a parting kiss, he was out of the door.

I sat on the couch, and Tré accompanied me. "You didn't want him to stay because I'm here? I didn't have a problem getting a room," he said.

"No, you're fine. Wesley doesn't stay the night here."

"Oh! So, you usually stay over at his place?" he asked, fidgeting with his phone.

"No. We don't spend the night together. We never have," I confessed.

Tré gave me an odd look, then started to frantically scroll through his phone. "What are you looking for?" I asked, confused by his behavior.

"I'm looking up the word *liar* to see if your picture is next to it! Come on, Ren! There's no way in the world a man will ask you to marry him and buy you a $100,000 truck without testing out the merchandise first, especially him! I know women throw themselves at him all the time! I see the comments on IG! I know his DM's have to be crazy! There's no way y'all haven't done anything! This is the same man who sang, and I quote, *Grind on my face, baby, drip down on me, and I'll show you the real meaning of ecstasy.*"

I laughed. "Well, little brother, obviously, your sister is the woman who he knew was worth waiting for. Grown men have restraint; boys don't. The right man will do what it takes for the right woman," I said, admiring my sparkling engagement ring.

"Well, whatever magic you put on him, no woman better not ever try to put on me! Cause I'm out!" he said. We both laughed.

"But for real, I'm happy for you, Ren. Wesley seems like a good dude, and he seems to make you happy. That's good enough for me. Congratulations."

My brother and I stayed up chatting until Wesley called. I ended my night talking to my future husband.

Over the next several weeks, Wesley and I began to make decisions about our wedding, like when, where, and how many guests. We decided we would get married in three months. We agreed on a small, intimate wedding and a luxurious honeymoon. Wesley's dad, my future father-in-law, offered to pay for our honeymoon as his gift to us. We hadn't yet decided where we would live, though. Wesley owned his house outright, and mine would be paid off in another few months. I still intended to keep working after we got married, and my job was only a fifteen-minute commute from my house. Wesley's house would add forty minutes to my morning commute, and the thought of that made me cringe. We agreed we would temporarily live in my house during the week and go to his house on the weekends after we were married until we figured things out.

Wesley also started working on making new music. He reached out to his former bandmates, and they decided they would record a new Xtascy album. He was excited to be back with his friends and doing what he loved. If all went well, they would be going on a small promo tour soon after the wedding.

Maya and Darren's bond had grown stronger than ever. She loved Ryan, Darren's son, and she got along fine with Darren's ex-wife. They were talking about moving in together and the possibility of expanding their family of three. I couldn't wait to walk down the aisle to become Mrs. Wesley Johnson Jr. I joked with Wesley that I'd thought about hyphenating my name, Serenity James-Johnson, and he said, as long as I said, "I do," I could call myself whatever I wanted!

I never did understand how brides-to-be got so stressed out when planning their weddings until now. It was a lot of work. There were so many little decisions that had to be made. I finally broke down and let Wesley hire us a wedding planner, so I could focus on the fun things like picking out my wedding dress, having a bachelorette party, and figuring out what I would do with my hair for our two-week honeymoon in Paris. Thank goodness for Maya and her event planning experience. As my maid of honor, she fielded several wedding planners' requests and issues before they ever got to me.

Chapter Thirty-Six

Wesley.

The wedding was a day away. I felt good but a little anxious. I didn't have cold feet because I knew marrying Serenity was the surest I'd been about anything in my life. The wedding planning was a little stressful, but we agreed on the majority of the details, including the number of guests that we narrowed down to just 150 people. At Dad's suggestion, Serenity and I completed five premarital counseling sessions with a therapist who was a longtime family friend, over the past few months. I'm glad we went. The sessions were insightful and helped us open up a whole new dialogue about our expectations and uncertainties about marriage. During one of the sessions, Serenity admitted she only had one sexual partner in her life, and that was her ex, Tony. Serenity said she met him in college, and they were together on and off for years. After things fell apart with him, she decided to practice celibacy. She said she never wanted to give herself to a man, or anyone, who didn't value her or know her worth. Serenity was usually like an open book, but when it came to the details of her ex, she froze up for some reason.

Since D was my best man, he was in charge of throwing my bachelor party. I wanted something low-key and tasteful. Much to my surprise, he rented out a pool hall for the men in the wedding party, and we had a stress-free night. I didn't know what Amaya planned for Serenity's bachelorette party, but she seemed like the type who would have a male stripper come in and turn up the festivities. I wasn't worried, though. I wanted Serenity to have fun and enjoy herself. "So, are you ready to take your final walk away from freedom in the morning?" D asked.

I sipped my beer. "No doubt," I answered without hesitation. I looked over at him. "And what about you? I know you've picked up on Amaya's not-so-subtle hints about wanting to get married. Y'all are already talking about having a baby. What's going on with that?" I asked, taking another swig of my drink.

"After my divorce, I'm really not in a rush to say 'I do' for the second time. I love her, and I don't want to be without her; I just want us to take a little more time. It's coming, though," D stated.

With everything going on, it was nice to blow off a little steam before the nuptials. Pop, D, Tré, Mr. James, and my three group members from Xtascy, Blue, Johnny and Marcell, rounded out the men who were there to celebrate.

"So, Wesley, since you're about to be my new brother and everything, why don't you see if you can hit up one of those model chicks to be my date tomorrow for the wedding? I know you got connections! Hook me up!" Tré requested, with a smile telling me he was serious. D and I laughed out loud at the young man's request. We both understood his angle because, after all, we were young men once. It had just been a long while since either of us was a wingman.

"I can't help you out with that one, youngin'! I'm almost a married man and reaching out to any woman asking them for a favor is not how I want to start," I joked.

He turned to D, with his hands up, seeing if he would oblige his request. "Sorry, lil' G, I can't help you, either! But, if you see someone you want to get at tomorrow, I'll put you up on game!" D offered.

"Alright! Good look!" Tré said as if he had just hit the lotto, walking off and catching up with his dad.

"Yo! That little cat is funny!" D said.

The rest of the night went well. We drank, talked smack, laughed, and reminisced on old times. I received marriage advice, some good and some questionable, and celebrated until close to midnight. Tomorrow was our wedding day, and I wanted to make sure I got ample sleep. I wanted to be well-rested and ready for the future Mrs. Johnson. We would go back to my house after the wedding because I wanted the first time I made love to my wife to be in our home. I had my whole bedroom and ensuite bathroom redone to remove any bad energy from my past. I did not want any of that energy in that space. I also got a huge clawfoot bathtub installed once Serenity told me how much she loved taking bubble baths. The following day, we would be catching a mid-morning flight to Paris to enjoy our honeymoon.

D and Tré stayed at my house for the night. We would arrive together at the church in the morning. It was 1:12 a.m. when I dialed her number. "Hello?" Serenity answered in a sleepy tone.

"Hey, baby, did I wake you?" I asked, whispering for some reason.

"I was just falling asleep. How was your bachelor party? Did you make it rain with a stack of ones? Cause I know Darren is about that life!" she asked, chuckling.

I smiled. "It was nice. No strippers! Nobody making it rain, just an easy time at the pool hall. Nothing big. How was your party? Who did Amaya have jumping out of cakes for you? Cause I know she's definitely about that life! I can hear her now, 'Tonight's your last night as free woman, Renny! Turn up!'" I laughed, doing my best impression of Amaya.

Serenity laughed, too. "I'm gonna tell her you're making fun of her! But, no, Wesley. No strippers," she said in a sweet tone. "We talked, and cried, and opened gifts—

some gifts I can use for our wedding night. My mom gave me some advice and —"

"Gifts for our wedding night?" I interrupted.

I'll admit, courting Serenity had been an experience I wouldn't trade for anything. By removing sex from the equation, we had no choice but to really see one another for who we were. I came to value and appreciate that experience because it forced me to explore other methods of expressing my affection toward her. I learned to love her in ways that a physical touch could never compete with. I loved her soul, mind, spirit, and heart. She loved me through my growth of becoming the man I wanted to be for her. She never forced me to do anything or presented me with ultimatums. She just loved me through every phase of love I traveled to reach the barriers I held in my heart.

She didn't knock down the walls I had built to protect my heart. I gladly removed them for her. She gave me 100 percent of her heart. In return, I wanted to do the same. Not having sex became a norm for us. I couldn't lie and say I didn't think about it, especially with those form-fitting dresses and heels and little yoga pants she walked around in. We tried to spend the night together a couple of times, but it was just too much for me. I knew I wouldn't be able to keep my hands off of her after the first ten minutes. Even though we were fully dressed, the way she smelled alone had me on ten.

I spent a lot of time in my home gym, working out to help get some of my pent-up energy out. I was in the best shape of my life! I wanted to make our wedding night special for her. I realized this would be the only chance I would have to make love to my wife for the first time. I imagined what it would feel like to experience her, several hundred times. However, I knew she wanted to honor the commitment she made to herself, so that meant I wanted to honor it, too.

Serenity snickered. "Yes, our wedding night, Wesley. In less than twenty-four hours," she said with a smile I could hear through the phone. I didn't know what to say because I didn't want to get myself too ramped up before needing to go to sleep, so I settled and said, "I can't wait to see it."

"Wesley," she said, sounding serious. "I've told you before that I had a big crush on you when I was younger. You were the cute boy on TV, and I was one of many who wished I could be your girlfriend. I literally used to daydream about what it would be like to meet you. I thought about what I would say, what I'd be wearing, and wishing you would see me, and instantly fall in love with this little ol' girl from Virginia!" she said and laughed. "I bought all of y'all's albums and faithfully watched every Xtascy video when it came on. I wanted to be one of y'all's video girls! You were every girl's fantasy, but you seemed so far away, like I would never be able to touch you. I never would have thought in one hundred years that any part of my fantasies about you would be my actual reality. The fact that you love me makes me sometimes, still, feel like I'm in that fantasy, and you're going to realize I am just a regular girl. I feel like one day I'm going to wake up, and this will all have been a dream. I want you to be 100 percent sure I'm who you want."

I took a long pause. "A video girl, huh?" I chuckled. "Serenity, you may have dreamt about meeting me back then, but I'm glad you didn't. I wouldn't have been ready to receive someone who had the makings of the woman you are today. Back then, all I cared about was making music, getting money, and meeting women. I would have squandered an opportunity with someone like you. You're not regular at all. You're exceptional. You're phenomenal, and meeting you fulfilled my fantasy before I even knew what it was. The way you love me with your whole heart is something I've never felt before. You love me, not my success, not my celebrity, not my money, you love *me*. I'm the one who is in awe of you. I'm the one who had to step up to meet you at your level to become worthy of your love. I have no doubts you are who I want, and I'm going to do the best I can to be a good husband to you, baby. I've never been so ready for anything in my life. You're the best thing to ever happen to me. I'm glad I slid into your DM's! I'm in love with you. Please, don't ever doubt that."

I heard her sniffling on the other end of the line. "I'm so in love with you, too, Wesley," she whispered, with her voice cracking.

"Don't cry, baby. Get some sleep," I said in a calming voice. "I'll see you tomorrow at the altar, 10:30 sharp."

"I'll be the one in the white dress."

✳✳✳✳✳

Serenity.

I had just fallen asleep after talking to Wesley. The buzzing sound of my phone woke me up. I found my phone under the mess of my blankets and in the darkness of my room. I adjusted my eyes to look at the screen. *Why is he calling me?* "Hello?" I answered in a voice that was still asleep.

"I'm sorry to wake you," Julian stammered.

"Julian, it's almost 2:30 in the morning. What's going on?" I asked, a little concerned but mostly irritated.

"I'm outside. Can you come out here for a minute," he whispered?

"You're at my house?!" I asked, pulling the blanket off of me and getting up to look out of my window. "What are you doing here?" I asked him, now starting to wake up.

"I just need to talk to you. It's important."

"Julian, this is not a good time—" I started to say, before he cut me off.

"It will only take a minute. Please, Serenity," he begged.

"Give me a minute." I ended the call. I had a house full of people who were attending the wedding in the morning and we would all be up in a few hours. The last thing I wanted to do was wake anyone. I was able to get out of the front door without alerting any of my guests. I walked down to the end of the driveway where Julian waited for me, anxiously leaning against his car. "Julian, what's going on?" I asked, tightening my floor length cotton robe around me. He lowered his head and took a deep breath.

"Are you sure about marrying him today?"

I scowled at him. "Seriously, Julian?! This is what you came here to say eight hours before my wedding? I can't believe you! I don't have time for this!" I angrily began to walk back towards my house. He grabbed my arm to stop me.

"Hey, I'm sorry! I'm not trying to make you upset," he paused, "It's just that I want to make sure that this is what you really want." He had a look of worry in his eyes.

"Julian, I love Wesley. I'm *in love* with Wesley and he's in love with me. I'm happy with him, and we're getting married today. That's all there is to it! What difference does it make to you anyway?" I kept my voice low so I wouldn't wake anyone sleeping inside.

"Okay. I get it. He's the fantasy guy. He's famous, he has the money, the looks, the cars… all of that, but he's not built to love you the way I can … The way I do. Serenity, I still feel you in my soul and I can't shake it. I've had to sit back all these months and watch him put a smile on your face, and I kept my distance because I knew it was the right thing to do. But I wouldn't be able to live with myself if I didn't at least try."

"Try what?!" My question silenced him. "Julian, I'm not doing this with you! I can't believe you even have the nerve to show up to my house in the middle of the night, and question how the man I'm going to marry loves me! Are you drunk or something? Are you crazy?"

He seemed to find my questions a bit amusing, which made me even angrier. I began to walk back up the driveway to go back into the house. He hurried to stand in front of me, blocking my exit. "Julian, move!" I demanded. He held his hands together as if he were ready to say a prayer.

"I told you before, Serenity, if you ever need me for anything, I'm here. That's not going to change. I'm sorry that I've upset you." I looked up at him and the look in his eyes told me that he believed every word he said. My heart softened a bit.

"Julian, let's just forget this ever happened, okay? It's late, I'm tired… this is a lot." His dark eyes peered down on me as if he were trying to choose his next words. However, he just nodded and moved to the side. I walked past him and went back into my house, quietly closing the door behind me. His words stirred me, but I didn't want to think about them or him.

"Was that Julian out there?" Maya's voice startled me in the dark. I turned on a lamp in the living room.

"Yes. And please, don't ask," I begged.

"Okay. I won't." She turned on her heels and headed back down the hall to the guest room. I laid back in bed and did my best to forget about Julian's attempt to place doubt in my head about Wesley. I had none. Within 24 hours, I was going to be Mrs. Wesley David Johnson Jr., and I couldn't wait.

Chapter Thirty-Seven

Serenity.

My mother and Maya helped me with my finishing touches. I usually insisted on minimal makeup. But for my wedding day, I had gotten a full beat. I had my hair done in long faux locs, which were expertly pinned up in an elegant updo. My dress was a simple yet stunning, pearl white strapless, full-length, mermaid-styled gown with a four-foot train. I opted not to wear a veil; instead, I wore a delicate headdress that laid slightly below my hairline. The bridal party was picture perfect, and the guests were already seated. Maya had to comfort my mother, who couldn't stop crying all morning. She had to get her makeup touched up at least three times because of her tears. There was a knock on the door. The wedding coordinator popped in her head and said, "It's time."

The bridal party entered first while my dad and I waited at the end of the line. I wanted to see Wesley so badly that I thought about breaking tradition and running down the aisle. When the bridal march played, my dad squeezed my arm while holding back tears. "You look so beautiful, baby girl," he whispered, as we entered the chapel.

"Thank you, Daddy," I said, smiling at the first man to ever hold my heart.

In a room full of family and friends, the only person I saw was Wesley. I had never seen him look so good. He had on a tailored black tux, along with the rest of the groomsmen. Seeing him filled my chest with a warmth that only he could ever give me. When we locked eyes, I saw his eyes begin to fill with tears. One fell, and he swiped it away before it was replaced with another. Darren patted him on his back and whispered something to help keep him keep his composure; but his eyes never left mine.

When asked by the pastor, my father gave me away. The pastor initiated the ceremony, and all we could do was look at one another. I wiped a few more tears from Wesley's eyes. I was surprised at how well I was able to hold back my own. After the pastor initiated the ceremony, he announced, "Wesley and Serenity have chosen to write their own vows. Serenity," he said, giving me the floor.

Wesley and I held hands. I took a deep breath and said, "Wesley, I've never known a love like this. You came into my life at a time when I wasn't sure I could love again. Your love opened my heart, and now, I can't imagine my life without loving you. You are my missing piece. You make everything in my life feel more complete, and full. I love you with everything in me. I vow to be your wife, best friend, confidant, partner, and lover. I promise to always give my love, heart, and body to only you. I vow to always be faithful and honor and respect you. I promise to hold you up and stand by you through everything, no matter what. You are my light, and because of you, my heart now shines like a beacon that would be visible from the bottom of the sea. I'm yours today and from this day forth."

At this point, there were not many dry eyes in the building. Darren pulled a handkerchief from the inside pocket of his jacket and wiped Wesley's tears away, a true show of brotherhood. Wesley gained his composure, cleared his throat, and said, "Serenity, thank you for choosing to love me. You are my heartbeat. There's nothing on this earth I wouldn't do for you. Your love has always been patient and kind, even when I know I didn't deserve it. Your love taught me how to love, and now, loving you is all I know. I thank God every day for the blessing that is you. As your husband, I will do everything I can to protect you, comfort you, and be everything you need me to be. My love for you is truly unconditional and unwavering, and there's no force on earth strong enough to break it. I promise to be your faithful husband, friend, and lover. I will cherish and honor you every day of our lives. I vow to always love you and only give myself to you from this day forth. You truly are my *serenity*."

We exchanged rings. Maya blotted my eyes to keep my face dry. "I think there's nothing more to say after that!" the pastor joked. "By the power vested in me, from the state of North Carolina, I now pronounce you husband and wife. Ladies and gentlemen, I now present to you, Mr. and Mrs. Wesley David Johnson, Jr. Wesley, you may now kiss your bride."

Wesley and I smiled at one another as he took a small step toward me and kissed me so deeply and passionately, that I wanted to skip the reception and go straight to our wedding night! Everyone cheered and whistled.

The guests exited the chapel while the wedding party took more photos. We arrived at the reception hall, and the whole ride over, Wesley and I made out like teenagers in the back of the car. I couldn't believe the day had finally come and I was now somebody's wife. My dress was like Fort Knox, and Wesley did not want to damage it by being too rough. "Don't worry, we got all night," I assured him.

"We have the rest of our lives," he countered.

After a quick change, we were announced again to the awaiting guests in the ballroom as Mr. and Mrs. Wesley David Johnson, Jr. to Marvin Gaye's hit song, "Got to Give it Up." We had our first dance, cut the cake, tossed the bouquet and the garter, and did the required electric slide. I was talking to our guests when Wesley, Johnny, Blue, and Marcell, otherwise known as the singing group Xtascy, entered the dancefloor and grabbed everyone's attention.

They had all changed into sneakers and stood in a formation that said they were ready to perform. This was unexpected because they hadn't performed together publicly in ten years, so this was going to be a treat.

"Baby, when I met you, you told me your favorite Xtascy song was "You Are," so this is for you," he said over the microphone. They began to sing a magnificent acapella rendition of the song, which pulled tears from my eyes. Wesley motioned for me to come up and join him, and he held my hand while singing the song to perfection. I sometimes forgot how phenomenal of a singer he truly was until he started to sing. Everyone in the group looked handsome, and time seemed to season their voices to precision. They sounded phenomenal.

Once the song was finished, everyone applauded. We kissed. His kisses were always the best, no matter how quick. I went back to join the rest of the guests. "You know, I can't have my boys up here with me and only do one song?" Wesley said, hyping up the crowd. The DJ dropped the beat for their biggest up-tempo song called "Dance Tonight." The crowd went even crazier, rushing people to the edge of the dancefloor.

Maya came to my side and said, "Girl, you know we got to dance to this one!" We watched the gentleman perform their song in all their boyband glory, and their choreography was still as tight as it had been years ago. Maya and I knew this choreography by heart and were encouraged by the guests surrounding us to go and join the fellas and dance with them.

"Oh, okay! Let's see what y'all got! Let's see if y'all are real Xtascy fans!" Johnny said over the microphone as Maya and I crept onto the dancefloor with the group. The guests cheered in anticipation. Wesley and the guys stood back, smiling big while the music still played.

"Bring it back to the chorus!" Maya yelled, making all four members of the group laugh. Wesley signaled the DJ to bring the chorus back around, and once they began singing the chorus again, Maya and I hit our eight-count like we created the dance.

After we hit our last step, we held up our hands to the group like we wanted to battle. The guests went crazy, and the guys began to bow down to show they were conceding. Then the DJ played the song's album version, and we all began pulling people onto the dancefloor. It quickly turned into a club scene. I saw my parents dancing together, Darren had found Maya, and even Tré was doing his little two-step with some woman looking way too old for him. Wesley grabbed me from behind and grinded all of him against me. He danced offbeat; I knew this dance with him wasn't about the song. It was an invitation. We had danced several times before, but he had never been so bold to press himself on me like this. My legs weakened, and the center of me became hot as I felt his undeniable desire for me. All I thought about was leaving the reception to have my night with my husband.

Chapter Thirty-Eight

Wesley.

I carried her into the candlelit bedroom. Soft music played; the air smelled sweet like fresh flowers. I placed Serenity on her feet and kissed her as deeply as I had hours ago after we were pronounced husband and wife. I was so calm, so in control. On the other hand, she wasn't interested in controlling her desire, evidenced by her unbuttoning my shirt and placing her tongue on my chest. I held her hands and whispered, "Mrs. Johnson." I kissed her hand. "My love, my bride, my queen. I want tonight to be special for you." I kissed her again. "Come with me," I directed.

I led her to my large ensuite bathroom, which was now *our* bathroom, where the lights were dim, and the music still played. I let go of her hand to turn on the water and started filling the tub. I poured bath salts, scented oil, and bubble bath in the water and topped it off with rose petals. I pulled a bench up to the side of the tub while it filled. "Come here," were my only two words to her. She obeyed. I rubbed her legs and looked up at her. She looked like a goddess. *Damn, I love this woman.*

"I want to bathe you, baby. Is that okay?" I asked, lacing kisses to her stomach through the chiffon fabric of her reception dress that she looked so good in that I barely wanted to take it off of her. She nodded. I turned her around and held her hips, squeezing them before slowly unzipping her dress. I sighed, knowing this would take more restraint than I probably had in me. I'd imagined what it would feel like to undress her a million times by now. She turned back to face me, slipping down her dress, revealing the black lace bra and panties she wore for me.

"You're stunning," I said, giving more kisses to her tight thighs. I reached behind her to unhook her bra, never breaking eye contact as it hit the floor. Her hands raised to cover her chest for some reason. At that moment, I remembered she once told me how she was constantly teased about the size of her chest. She said she had even considered getting implants at one point because she felt so insecure about it. I moved her hands. "Don't do that. Every part of you is perfect," I said because it was true.

Next, I slid her panties down, and she stepped out of them. I kissed the inner V of her thighs and stroked her with my thumbs. She now stood before me, completely naked for the first time. Her body was like art. Her stomach was toned and tight; her breasts were perfectly round and perky. Her sun-bathed skin already smelled sweet, and she had the softest skin I'd ever felt. I wrapped my hands to the back of her, squeezing two handfuls of her backside. She moaned and grabbed the nape of my neck, leaned over, and kissed me, eagerly feeding me her tongue. The bathtub was just about filled, and I helped her in. I took off my shirt, now only wearing an undershirt and slacks. I began to bathe my wife. The music and her breaths were all the soundtrack I needed for the night. I took a large loofah sponge and made small circles on her back, neck, arms, chest, legs, and feet. "Mmmmm," she sighed.

I gently massaged her shoulders and breasts; her eyes closed in pleasure. I leaned over to kiss her lips. She looked so content. "You soak. I'm going to get cleaned up down the hall. I'll be back," I whispered. In the guest bathroom, I showered and changed into a black terry cloth robe, then headed back to the master bedroom. I saw the balcony doors were open when I walked back into the room. The warm air and the sounds of the night played on my senses. My eyes were drawn to her—my forever love. She sat on the chaise lounge chair, sipping champagne, and stood when I entered. She had on a red, sheer lace bodysuit with red heels that had to be at least four inches high.

"I've been waiting for you," she said in a voice so sexy that I couldn't believe it came from her. Seeing my wife in red lingerie was something I hadn't asked for, but I was still thankful.

"Oh, yeah?" I asked while my lustful eyes played over her body.

"Come here," she commanded. "There's something I've been wanting to give you."

I walked over to her, not needing an invitation, but I played along. She untied my robe as I took her lips and tongue into my mouth. "You taste so good, baby," I said, returning to her lips. Her hands navigated down to my shaft, and she gently stroked me. The feel of her sent a wave up my spine. I kissed her deeper, lifting her by the legs and heading over to the bed. I felt her wetness pressed against my stomach and my knees buckled for a moment at the sensation. I laid her down on the satin sheets and began kissing and licking her neck and chest. Her crotchless garment granted my fingers access to her now dripping center. "Oh, my goodness," I mumbled at the discovery of how wet she was for me. I licked my fingers clean, and the taste of her made me grow hungrier for her. She didn't know it yet, but she would soon find out I was gluttonous in the bedroom. I overindulged every chance I got, and now that she was my wife, I had nothing left to hold back. "Tell me what you want tonight. I want to give you exactly what you want. Just tell me. I'll do anything to please you," I panted, putting my lips on her stomach and kissing her through the sheer fabric of her lingerie.

"I want all of you. You can do whatever you want to me. I'm yours forever," she panted.

I rose back up to her lips, kissing her without restraint. I became intoxicated by the taste of her. She wrapped her legs around my waist, encouraging me to enter her. I saw a slight look of worry in her eyes. I knew it had been at least two-and-a-half years since she'd been with anyone, and it had been over a year for me, so I knew I had to take it slow. I didn't want to hurt her or finish too quickly. "I'll take my time with you, baby. Tell me if it's too much, okay?" I asked.

She nodded. Maintaining eye contact, I gradually made my way inside her walls. She gasped, slightly arching her back. I let out a hard groan when the full length of me entered her for the first time. "Damn, baby!" I knew she would feel good, but I wasn't prepared for this. Serenity weakened me. She was super tight, soaking wet and hot. I had never felt anything quite like this before. She had a grip on me like I'd never experienced. Her walls sucked me back in every time I pulled back to stroke her.

When I began to go a little deeper and harder, I saw a tear fall from the corner of her eye. I slowed down and asked, "Does it hurt, baby?"

"No— I just never made love before," she sobbed. I knew what she meant because I felt the same way. She wasn't a woman I would be sending home in a couple of hours or one I'd promise to call and never did. She was my wife, and I wanted her to feel love every time I touched her.

"I love you," I said, keeping my strokes steady with her thigh gripped beneath one hand, while the other hand palmed her breast. Her heavy breaths turned into loud, gratifying moans while she dug her nails into my back. It was like she was singing to me the best song ever written, and I was the musician. She wrote the lyrics, and I played the melody. "I ain't never felt something so good, baby! My God you feel so good!" I whispered in her ear. I fed my tongue to her, muting her moans. She tightened her walls on me, causing me to stall for half of a second. *What the hell was that?*

Then she did it again. She began tightening around me in intervals as I stroked her. I was trying my best not to lose my mind, but everything about her and this moment aroused me beyond reasonable thoughts. "Baby!" I groaned, finding myself on the cusp of calling out her name. She brought me to the edge, and I was ready to jump over it. I pulled out. "Take this off. Leave them heels on, though," I commanded, wanting to feel her skin to skin. "Rollover," was my next command. She laid on her stomach, whimpering my name when I entered her once again. I dotted kisses on the back of her neck and shoulders while my arms stayed firmly planted on the sides of her. I stroked her slowly, almost pulling out before gliding back in with ease. I wanted her to feel every inch of me.

"It's so big! You feel so good! Please, don't stop! Wesley!" she cried out. It was game over. Her words did it for me. I pounded into her fast and hard, showing her no mercy.

"Take it, baby! It's all for you! Take all of it!" I rumbled in her ear. She cried out in passion-filled screams, burying her face in the mattress and gripping the sheets. I released myself into her with a few final strokes and a loud grunt of my own before collapsing on top of her. I rolled onto my back to catch my breath. I pulled my wife to my chest, rubbing her back and kissing her forehead. "I love you," I said into the dim room.

Chapter Thirty-Nine

Serenity.

I removed myself from the hold of his arms as he slept nestled behind me. We had made love three more times, and each time was better than the last. Making love to Wesley had been well worth the wait, and he was more than I expected. Actually, he exceeded everything I dreamed it would be. He did not lack in size, strength, or stamina. After our first time, I was certain of why his ex, Candice, went crazy when they broke up. Honestly, I couldn't understand why she would even go looking for anything better. None of that mattered now, anyway. He hadn't heard from her in close to a year. He did hear some chatter that she had moved back to Georgia to stay with her mother. Apparently, someone had a medical issue, and she went there to help out for a little while. Either way, I was glad she hadn't tried to disrupt his life again.

We needed to be up in a few hours to catch our flight to Paris for our honeymoon. He pulled me back onto him. "Where are you going?" he asked, half asleep.

"Bathroom," I answered, prompting him to release me.

I looked in the bathroom mirror before returning to the bedroom to join my sleeping husband. My eyes looked different. They were peaceful and calm. I walked over to the bed and looked down at my exhausted husband. He looked like the closest thing to a perfect man that I had ever seen. His rich chocolate skin, handsome face, full lips and muscular body called out to me. Now that we had explored the physical side of our love, my desire for him went to ten onsite.

I got back in the bed and nudged him until he rolled over on his back. "Baby," he sighed, sounding sleepy. "Give me a minute." I straddled him, kissing his chest and moving down to lick his nicely defined stomach, gently nibbling on him. He took in a quick breath through his teeth.

"I want to take care of you," I said, taking the whole of him between my lips. His strength began to wake up from my actions, and his breaths deepened. I hadn't done this in a while, but I felt like I was doing it the way he liked based on his body movements and the profanities he let leave his lips. He gripped the back of my head, guiding me into a rhythm he desired.

"Yes, just like that," he coached. I moaned and genuinely craved the taste of him. His passion was building by the moment. I felt it. His body was starting to tense up and his toes curled and cracked while his sounds of pleasure became more audible. I was on the verge of completing my mission when he said, "Come here." I released him from my mouth and climbed his body, meeting his lips with mine. "Give me another taste of that. Have a seat right here," he said, licking his lips and melting me with those grayish-blue eyes that seemed to look right through me. Even in the dark, I could see them. My knees sank on the sides of his head, and he locked them in place with his arms. I grabbed the headboard in front of me. I had a feeling I would need it. He savored me. I had never felt any pleasure as mind-blowing as what he was able to give me. This pleasure came from love, and my body reacted accordingly.

"Yes! Right there!" I screeched in pure bliss.

"Mm hmm," he grumbled beneath me. He transported me to another dimension through a series of screams and moans. *This was ecstasy.* He lowered my limp body on to his awaiting member, who was still at attention. He held me tight around my back, pressing me against his chest while he thrust his pelvis into me harder and faster. My voice had gone missing, leaving me only to pant uncontrollably. "Oh my God!" he relented in a voice so deep, it gave me a surge of energy to meet his stroke. Our peaks met one another once again, being subdued with our tongues dancing with one another.

✳✳✳✳✳

We had to be at the airport by 9:00 a.m. for our 11:15 flight to Paris. We had one layover in Atlanta, and our travel time was a little over ten hours. I had never been to France, and I reveled at the thought of spending our first two weeks married overseas. Wesley had been to Paris a few times when he was touring, but he hadn't been back in several years since. We agreed to visit all the popular tourist attractions like the Eiffel Tower and the Cathedral of Notre Dame while we were there. I was so in love with Wesley and I could still hardly believe we had gotten married. We stayed glued to one another. I'm sure anyone looking on could tell we were newlyweds. We flew first class and enjoyed champagne, strawberries, and steak dinners during the final leg of our flight. Our hotel suite was immaculate. Wesley's dad had spared no expense when he gifted us this trip. I didn't even want to know how much our room cost. I'm sure the financial advisor in me would have winced in disapproval.

We spent the first three days of our honeymoon making love all morning and all night, all over our suite. We only left the hotel room to eat, giving housekeeping a chance to replenish our amenities. We were in our own little bubble. We couldn't get enough of one another. We indulged in one another without regard for exploring the beautiful city that waited outside our window. We fed one another bites of food at every meal and any stretch of time we had to be apart felt too long. Our late-night private pool parties always turned into intense make-out sessions like we were lovesick teenagers. Our kisses were always followed by the most fiercely uninhibited love making encounters either one of us could stand. We were in love. We were in Paris, and this had to be the best I'd ever felt in my life.

On the fourth day, we went out sightseeing and did a little shopping because Paris was too beautiful to not explore it. Wesley insisted that I take his Black Card and get myself whatever I wanted. However, when I saw a purse I liked, it was $12,000! And that was one of the cheap ones! I didn't get it because there was no way I could ever justify such an extravagant purchase. However, the next day when I got out of the shower, the purse I'd been admiring was waiting for me on the nightstand with a note saying: *You deserve everything you want and more. I love you, Wesley.*

I can't forget to mention the food! Wesley's new hobby of cooking led him to research different restaurants he wanted to try. I ordered what he suggested and was pleasantly surprised by how much I enjoyed most of the dishes. He made me laugh when he asked to speak to the chef in an attempt to get their secret recipes and techniques. The language barrier itself was humorous. We took so many photos and videos during our trip that we had memories to last us a lifetime.

The days and nights went by quickly, and before we knew it, we were on our last day in Paris. We spent the afternoon at Disneyland being carefree and reminiscing on our childhoods. That turned out to be my favorite day in Paris. "Time to go back to reality tomorrow," I said as Wesley, and I sat in the hot tub on the roof of the hotel.

"It'll be alright, baby," he said, kissing me on my cheek.

"Can you believe we've been married for two weeks already?" I asked, smiling at my undeniably handsome husband.

"Yeah, time is flying." We looked up at the night sky and enjoyed the sound of silence. We enjoyed the peace of being with one another. I knew there was nowhere else in this world I would have rather been than with him.

Chapter Forty

Wesley.

We touched down in Charlotte around 7:00 p.m. on Saturday. We had to get back into the swing of things, and we were eager to find our rhythm as a married couple. Cohabitating and traveling between two different homes would be a challenge. Serenity would have to go back to work Monday morning, and I would be going back to the studio to work on the new album with the fellas. But for now, I just wanted to sit down and rest. I hired a maid to come in and clean once a week. She also checked the mail for me while I was gone. "Home sweet home, baby," I smiled and kissed Serenity, pulling back and licking my lips.

She looked up. "Don't start," she quipped. "We just got here!"

She gave me a look I couldn't quite read. "What's wrong?" I asked, still smiling at the fact that this was now her home, too, as we entered the house through the garage.

"Nothing," she said, suspiciously. I narrowed my eyes at her. She sighed, "There's a couple bags in the living room I meant to bring on our honeymoon. Would you mind grabbing it for me?" She asked, with a flirtatious stare.

"Is it lingerie?" I asked, already picturing her in it.

"Yes, and maybe I can try on a couple of them for you tonight," she said, giving me her bedroom eyes.

"Say no more!" I rolled in our luggage and placed them by the stairs, but something else caught my eye. I walked into the living room and turned on the lights. My heart nearly dropped down to my feet. "Baby!" I yelled, not knowing which emotion would leave my throat. I turned to find Serenity who stood behind me with the biggest smile I'd ever seen her wear. "You did this?" I asked, in disbelief. She nodded.

"I wanted to get you a wedding present; something you would actually use. Your dad helped me pick it out and Darren came here when it was delivered. Remember when you had trouble with your security camera app last week and I convinced you it was just a glitch? It was because I wanted this to be a surprise."

I hugged her, lifting her from her feet, and sprinkling her with kisses. "Thank you, baby," I whispered. "No one has ever done anything like this for me before. I love you so much."

"You're welcome," she said, with tears forming in her eyes. Go and check it out!" She encouraged.

I took a moment to take in the brand-new Steinway Model B Grand Piano that sat in our living room. It was beautiful. It had an African Pommele wood finish and gold accents. I walked up to it and touched it to make sure it was real. "You have to get these pianos made to order. It can take up to a year to get one of these. How did you do this soon quickly?" I asked, still in shock from her generous gift.

"It wasn't easy! But I know people who know people. It's one of the perks of my job. I was just hoping you would like it." She looked down, "I just want to make you as happy as you make me."

I sat down on the lush, tufted piano bench and motioned for Serenity to join me. She sat next to me and fixed her eyes on mine. I knew a kiss, a hug, or an 'I love you,' did not properly describe how I felt in this moment. I couldn't put my own words together for this level of intensity coursing through me. This was the most thoughtful and generous gift anyone has ever gotten me. She leaned on my shoulder. "Play something for me," she murmured. Instantly, I knew that "Never Felt This Way" by Brian McKnight would be the perfect song for the mood. Still wearing our jackets and shoes we traveled in, I played my piano and sang to the love of my life. I hoped every word I sang kissed her in ways that represented my love.

✳✳✳✳✳

Once we finally made it upstairs, we spent the next forty-five minutes calling our families and friends and telling them about our honeymoon. We were exhausted and in bed by ten o'clock. Even in my exhaustion, I still joined Serenity in the shower, devouring every part of her body under the hot stream of water; giving her the proper thank you she deserved. After all, it was still our honeymoon.

The next morning, after breakfast, Serenity headed back over to her house to get ready for her work week and catch up with Amaya. I told her I'd be there by dinner time because I was going to visit Pop and D today. When she left, I went to my office to look at my schedule for the week and check emails since I'd been gone for two weeks,

I had to spend long hours in the studio so we could finish our album on time. I saw our wedding photos had come in, but the video would take another week or so. I felt butterflies in my stomach thinking back to that day and how perfect Serenity looked. Another email caught my attention, *"The State of Georgia?"* I read aloud. I opened the email, and the contents made my stomach flip. There was a number to call. But it was the weekend, so no one answered. I checked my mail because requests like this usually came in the mail, right? "This has to be fake," I said to myself over and over again. I grabbed my keys and headed over to Serenity's house. She hadn't been there long before I arrived. When I busted in, she was on the couch, talking to Amaya. They both turned to me with a look of concern on their faces.

"Wesley is everything okay?" she asked, standing and walking over to me.

I was sweaty, and my stomach churned. "I need to talk to you right now. It's important," I said. Then I turned to Amaya. "I'm sorry for being rude, Amaya. I just need her for a few minutes."

We went to the bedroom and closed the door. I sat down on the bed and dropped my head. "Wesley, you're starting to scare me," she said, looking nervous. "What's going on? Whatever it is, I'm here for you."

I sighed, "I don't know how clse to say this, but I'm being petitioned for a paternity test by Candice." I handed her the notice that came in the mail last week. She sat down next to me and looked it over. Candice had given birth to a baby girl who she named Sky Imari Douglas, who was now three-and-a-half months old. Having a baby would explain why she suddenly disappeared and completely dropped off everyone's radar.

"Wait," Serenity said, shaking her head. "You said she took five pregnancy tests in LA, and they were all negative! What the hell is this?" she asked, raising her voice for the first time since I'd known her.

"I don't know! I don't know anything about this! I haven't talked to her since that day! I didn't know she had a baby!"

"Did you watch her take those tests, Wesley?" My head began to throb.

"No. She went into the bathroom for fifteen minutes and came out with five negative tests. That's all that happened."

"Y'all didn't use protection?" she asked in a high octave.

"We did. We used condoms at first. But after we got tested, Candice said she was taking birth control. After that, we didn't use condoms as much," I answered, feeling like the biggest sucker in the world.

Serenity began to cry at the possibility of her new husband having a baby with another woman and with Candice, no less. I held her, trying to calm her, but she was inconsolable.

Amaya knocked on the bedroom door. "Renny? Wesley? Is everything okay in there?" she asked.

"Uhh, she's upset, but I got her," I yelled through the door, still trying to soothe my sobbing wife. "Baby, wait here." I got up to open the door. I stepped out and closed the door behind me. I held my hands to my face.

"Did someone die?" Amaya asked with a look of fear.

"No. But you should probably head home. I'll make sure she calls you later. I got her. I'll take care of her, okay?" I asked, trying to remain stoic.

"Okay, Wesley," Amaya agreed with reluctance. "Tell her to call me no matter what time it is."

"I will," I said, going back into the bedroom where Serenity was now stretched out over the bed.

My mind was a mess, and my heart was in shambles. I honestly didn't know what to do. Candice lied about being pregnant, and there was a baby that could be mine. I couldn't fathom why she would keep a pregnancy from me and why would she be seeking paternity now? I had to sort that out later. But now, I needed to tend to my wife. I slipped my shoes off and lay in the bed next to her, facing her wet eyes and vacant expression. "Serenity, I'm so sorry this is happening. We just need to take one step at a time. I need you by my side for this, baby. I need you." I whispered, wiping more fallen tears from her eyes.

She swallowed hard and said, "I'm here for you. It's just the possibility of it being true that scares me. I want to have your baby…" she stopped herself and sighed. "You're right. Let's just take one step at a time."

"I'll call to make an appointment tomorrow. But for now, I need you to be okay. Tell me what you need, and I'll do it for you," I said, kissing her forehead.

She sniffled and took a long pause. "Well, you could grab us some snacks from the kitchen so we can watch some trashy reality TV shows," she said, forcing a smile.

"Okay, I can do that. I need to make a few phone calls. But I'll be right back, okay?"

I closed the door behind me and blew out a hard breath, feeling like my legs wanted to give out. I called Pop and D to tell them I'd catch up with them later. Then I grabbed a few snacks from the kitchen and headed back to the bedroom. I walked back into the room to find Serenity balled up under her blanket in an effort to stifle her crying. The sight was like a kick to the face. I put the snacks down and pulled up the blanket to lay behind her. I held her tight, not knowing the right words of comfort to offer. "Everything will be okay," I said and repeated. I only hoped that everything *would* be okay.

To be continued…

~About the Author~

Kya Montague is a Southern New Jersey native who enjoys the beach, the sounds of the ocean and a good love story. She began writing short stories at age 7, and developed a love of writing poetry by her teenage years. In 2021, Kya debuted her first romance novel, "A Love Like This, Part 1," which has become a fan favorite. Since then, she has expanded her catalog while *'penning love stories, one character at a time.'* Staying true to her poetic roots, Kya loves to infuse the whimsical flair and thoughtful language of poetry into her novels.

In late 2023, Kya added on to her creative endeavors and started a podcast showcasing the immense talent in the Black literary community called, "The Mic'd Up Podcast." She finds immense joy in connecting with new readers and supporters of her creative ventures online and in-person.

She currently resides in Virginia where she's working on bringing more love stories to readers who never tire of falling in love with characters who are *falling in love*.

For business-related inquiries, please email me at:
Author.KyaMontague@outlook.com